The
WITCH'S
GUIDE
to COOKING *with* CHILDREN

The WITCH'S GUIDE

to COOKING *with* CHILDREN

KEITH McGOWAN

with illustrations by YOKO TANAKA

Christy Ottaviano Books

HENRY HOLT AND COMPANY • NEW YORK

Henry Holt and Company, LLC

Publishers since 1866

175 Fifth Avenue

New York, New York 10010

www.HenryHoltKids.com

Distributed in Canada by H. B. Fenn and Company Ltd.

Library of Congress Cataloging-in-Publication Data

McGowan, Keith.

The witch's guide to cooking with children / Keith McGowan ; illustrated by Yoko Tanaka. — 1st ed.

p.   cm.

"Christy Ottaviano Books."

Summary: Eleven-year-old inventor Sol must recover his self-confidence if he and
his eight-year-old sister, Connie, are to escape the clutches of Hansel and Gretel's witch,
to whom they have been led by their new stepmother and the man they believe is their father.

ISBN 978-0-8050-8668-3

[1. Brothers and sisters—Fiction. 2. Witches—Fiction. 3. Self-confidence—Fiction.
4. Inventors and inventions—Fiction. 5. Characters in literature—Fiction.
6. Germany—Fiction.] I. Tanaka, Yoko, ill. II. Title.

PZ7.M478487Wit 2009

[Fic]—dc22

2008050269

First edition—2009 / Designed by April Ward

Printed in July 2009 in the United States of America by
Quebecor World, Fairfield, Pennsylvania

1   3   5   7   9   10   8   6   4   2

For Angelika

The
WITCH'S
GUIDE
to COOKING *with* CHILDREN

From HÄNSEL UND GRETEL

by Jacob Grimm and Wilhelm Grimm

. . . Die Alte aber wackelte mit dem Kopfe und sprach: »Ei, ihr lieben Kinder, wer hat euch hierher gebracht? Kommt nur herein und bleibt bei mir, es geschieht euch kein Leid.« Sie faßte beide an der Hand und führte sie in ihr Häuschen. . . . Hänsel und Gretel legten sich hinein und meinten, sie wären im Himmel.

Die Alte hatte sich nur so freundlich angestellt, sie war aber eine böse Hexe, die den Kindern auflauerte, und hatte das Brothäuslein bloß gebaut, um sie herbeizulocken. Wenn eins in ihre Gewalt kam, so machte sie es tot, kochte es und aß es, und das war ihr ein Festtag.

. . . The old woman shook her head and said, "Aye, my dear children, who has brought you here? Come on in and stay with me, no harm will come to you." She took both by the hand and led them into her cottage. . . . Hansel and Gretel lay themselves down and thought they were in heaven.

But the old woman had only pretended to be nice. She was an evil witch. She waylaid children and had built the bread cottage simply to lure them in. Once they fell into her clutches, she finished them off, cooked them and ate them, and that was, for her, a merry holiday.

HOW TO COOK AND EAT CHILDREN
A Cautionary Tale by the Witch Fay Holaderry

I love children. Eating them, that is.

I've eaten quite a few children over the centuries. You may wonder where I get them all. The answer is: I get them the traditional way. From parents, of course. You'd be amazed how many parents have shown up at my hideaway with their children in tow. Or written to me on their best stationery, requesting that I take their children, "pretty please!" One group even rented a helicopter to find me and hand their children over. Daughters and sons they couldn't stand one second longer.

If only children knew.

I remember Derek Wisse, whose only fault, actually, was to fail math every year. Well, he was also a horrible speller.

His parents couldn't understand it. They were both geniuses. Mr. Wisse had an MD and a PhD, while Mrs. Wisse had two PhDs, one PhE, plus a very hard-to-get PhZ.

The Wisses didn't think it unreasonable that their child should be at least as smart as them.

"How can you be my son and not do well in school?" Mr. Wisse asked.

Mrs. Wisse was more sympathetic, but equally puzzled. "Why don't you try harder?" she pleaded with him.

But, try as he might, Derek couldn't succeed. He brought home D's and F's on every report card.

And those letters, unlike the ones Mr. and Mrs. Wisse had, weren't any good at all.

Derek was a great disappointment to his parents.

He didn't disappoint me, though . . . baked with secret ingredients and served with my very yummy homemade key lime pie.

And then there was Jane Markers, who foolishly gave one of her mother's expensive fur coats to a woman sleeping on the street. The woman seemed to need it more than her mother.

"How could you?" Mrs. Markers asked when she found out.

"But you have so many," reasoned Jane.

"Yes," Mrs. Markers said, "but THAT one was a birthday present from your stepfather. It was very special."

Jane shook her head. "Why can't you be more . . . what's that word?"

"Generous?" asked Mrs. Markers. "Well,

maybe I can," she said, considering it. "Yes, I'll try, Jane."

And, right after that, Mrs. Markers proved that she could be very generous after all.

Very generous to me, that is.

And I still remember Jeffrey Dach, centuries ago. Jeffrey's parents trained him from his earliest days to love music. They started him on violin lessons as soon as he was big enough to push down the strings. By age eight, he was a brilliant musician, headed for youthful fame—just as his parents had planned.

"One day soon, you'll be playing before the royalty of all the world," they told him. "Won't that be wonderful?"

Jeffrey's parents thought that it would. But then, one afternoon, he fell while climbing a tree in search of a ripe pear and broke his wrist. Just like that, Jeffrey's music career was over, and the Dachs' grand dreams were spoiled.

I, though, still saw great potential in Jeffrey, like how well he would turn out cooked with capsicum and washed down with a fine mead. Thanks to ME, Jeffrey lived up to that potential.

And recently there was rich Grant Feltwright, who thought he was better than everyone else because of his family's wealth.

He told his classmates, "My father could hire your parents as assistants." He bragged about family vacations scuba diving and skydiving. And he often won at sports, but only by tricking gullible kids into looking the wrong way at important moments. He thought that made him clever.

His father told him, "This is not the way you uphold the honor of the Feltwright name."

But Grant wouldn't listen. So Mr. Feltwright did what he needed to do to preserve the family name.

And I preserved Grant in vinegar, salt, and sodium metabisulfite.

I try to make it easy for parents to hand their

children over. That way I get more children. I have put up some child drop-off boxes in convenient locations, many near movie theaters. Children always want to go to the movies. Parents take them there and usually, to confuse the children, they buy them much more popcorn, candy, and soda than usual.

Then, when the movie's over, they lead their children out the side exit and quickly throw them into one of my giant metal boxes—labeled simply DONATIONS. These boxes have swinging doors at the top that open one way—IN—but not the other.

I also offer tours through my "Child-Friendly Travel Bureau," as well as special "hazardous children" pickup days four times a year. It's not like the old days. There's no more leading one's children into the forest. I don't live in the forest anymore. They've torn down the trees and built houses all around me. I've had to make my home look like all the rest—at least to the eyes. . . .

If you are a child and you are reading this, you may want to ask yourself a few questions. Do you demand unreasonable things from your parents? Do you always do what you are told? How often do you ask for a raise in your allowance? Have either of your parents said, anytime recently, one or more of the following things: "I'm at the end of my rope," "I'm sick and tired of your behavior," or, very important, "I can't take it anymore"?

If the answers to these questions are *Yes*, *No*, *A Lot*, and *Yes*, then you may want to consider changing your ways.

You might wonder why I would tell you this. Wouldn't that mean one less delicious meal for me? But I'm not afraid of warning you. Of course not. I understand children quite well. Not just how to season them delicately. Or what kind of side dishes go well with what kind of kids. I know all about not-yet-cooked children too. I know they have little self-control. I know that one day they'll decide to be good, and the next thing you know they'll forget all about it and get into trouble. They can't stick to their decisions. Their willpower is weak.

I always get them in the end.

I could get you too . . .

SO wrote Fay Holaderry one June night in a notebook titled "How to Cook and Eat Children: A Cautionary Tale." Holaderry's faithful cocker spaniel, J. Swift, lay at her feet. His snout rested easily on his front paw, his big round eyes occasionally glancing up at his mistress, raising his eyebrows, but not his head, to look up. Outside it was dark. Inside Holaderry's house, as she wrote, all was quiet. The only sound was that of Holaderry turning a page, or the sound of her picking at a snack from a plate in front of her. She had prepared the snack herself.

Delicious.

CHAPTER

SOL AND CONNIE

Monday

SOLOMON AND CONSTANCE Blink—Sol and Connie for short—moved into the town of Grand Creek one hot day in the middle of August. Sol was eleven and Connie was eight.

The late afternoon sun streamed over the mountains into Sol's new bedroom as he unpacked. He'd already taken out a telescope and a microscope. These allowed him to peer into other worlds, large and small, that sometimes seemed more appealing than this one.

He examined the instruments, his hand at his chin, his long hair falling in front of his shoulders.

He unpacked a box of science books next, checking their titles as he ordered and stacked them. Most of the books looked advanced, almost like what scientists might have had on their own shelves. Sol, you see, was a very smart boy.

His intelligence, however, hadn't helped to make him the number one most popular boy at his old school. Popular slots two to one hundred had also been taken.

Sol may have been remembering his old school just then, because his lips twisted into a grimace. Maybe he was even remembering his worst day ever. Last spring.

The Terrible Day . . .

He didn't know that an even more terrible day lay ahead for him.

The next box Sol opened held a curious device, which he removed carefully. The device was something he had made himself. It had a CPU—central processing unit—at center and an octopus of wires attaching the CPU to meters and a screen. That screen displayed, in order, the temperature, barometric pressure, time, and, based on all of that information, a guess at the current weather. The screen showed, "82°, 855 MB, 4:02PM," and "SUNNY," which were all correct.

Sol smiled and breathed a quiet snort. He set the device gently on the windowsill, then turned to his other boxes.

In one, he found his mother's old scientific treatise, yellowed and tattered. A talented scientist, Sol and Connie's mother had traveled many years before to study warming in the Antarctic. There she'd made a discovery of great importance: The ice shelf was melting at an alarming rate. Unfortunately, she discovered this while standing on the ice shelf, which, as predicted, melted and fell into the ocean. She was never heard from again. Though her results, radioed in, did survive and were hailed by the scientific world.

Sol spent a few minutes paging through his mother's work, then his eyes fell on the thing that lay below it, a plaque that his sister, Connie, had given him last spring. The plaque read: MANY OF LIFE'S FAILURES ARE PEOPLE WHO DID NOT REALIZE HOW CLOSE THEY WERE TO SUCCESS WHEN THEY GAVE UP— THOMAS EDISON. He turned the plaque facedown and placed it in a spare box with some old books.

After some time he confronted one unlabeled

box, all taped up, which he didn't open. Instead, he pushed it into the farthest reaches of his new closet, as if he never wanted to see it again.

Then he went out of the bedroom to see how the rest of the moving was going and what his younger sister was up to.

Connie was very different from her brother. She was outside the two-story apartment building at that moment beside the moving truck. She'd climbed onto her family's sofa as it was being picked up by two of the movers. So that the movers carried both the sofa and Connie across the lawn and into the small building, with Connie sitting up very queenlike and slowly waving, first left and then right, to an imaginary audience of onlookers. Those onlookers were, in her mind, watching her brilliant and important entrance being carried into her new home. In the hallway outside the apartment, one neighbor did open her door to look out. Connie honored the neighbor with a wave and an elegant nod.

To look at Connie enjoying herself that day, you would never have known that she was keeping a guilty secret from her brother. But then, you couldn't tell how much she missed her old cat, Quantum, either, and she missed Quantum very much. It wasn't that Connie didn't feel sad about her cat, or guilty about the secret she kept from her brother. It's just that she wasn't one to mope.

As to what she looked like, Connie was spry and flexible. She had very short hair and big ears that stuck out on either side of her small head, possibly made like that to let certain comments pass quickly into one and out the other, spending as little time as possible in between. Comments, for instance, like her father's outburst when the movers carried not just the sofa into the apartment but Connie too.

"Connie! Get off that couch this instant!" Mr. Blink said. Mrs. Blink—who had married Sol and

Connie's father just before the move—looked up from unpacking and shook her head in amazement.

Connie was the tiniest bit slow in responding to her father's order, though. So that she slid off the sofa just after the movers put it down, completing her grand ride in style.

Sol was coming out of the bedroom then and saw that his father and stepmother were upset. He ducked into the kitchen to pour himself a glass of ice water—it was very hot that Monday—then came out and said, "Connie, want to go to the park?"

Connie nodded.

"Dad, can we go?" he asked.

"Anything that gets you out of here," Mr. Blink answered, "is fine with me."

Sol and Connie found a Frisbee and a tennis ball in one of the boxes lying in the living room. Before they left, Sol saw his glass of ice water, now mostly ice, on the counter and had the idea to teach Connie something.

"Come look at this." He took her into the kitchen, poured some more water into the glass, and added a couple more ice cubes. "I'm going to mark the level of the water." He found some masking tape and used that to do it. "Now, when we get back and the ice has melted, will the water be higher than it is now, or lower?"

"Higher," Connie said.

"Why?"

"Because when the ice melts, there'll be more water, so the water will go up."

"Are you sure?"

"Yes."

"Are you willing to bet on it? Do you have any money?"

Connie checked. "Three dollars."

"Will you bet the three dollars?"

"Sure, I'll bet you three dollars the water'll be higher," she said stubbornly. "What do you say? You say it'll be lower?"

"Nope. I say it will be in exactly the same place after the ice melts. Want to take back your bet?"

"No!" Connie said, not one to give in. Connie also wasn't one to lose a bet, though, especially if it involved her own money. So she made sure to sneak back, as she and her brother were leaving, to pour just a little more water into the glass. Then she caught up with Sol. She suspected that he knew more about this scientific matter than she did. But he didn't know enough to win three dollars from her. Of that she was certain.

CHAPTER

SCIENTIFIC CURIOSITY

SOL AND CONNIE'S new block was a street of houses with their own small apartment building at one end—a two-story building that held six apartments. As the children stepped outside, the movers were still working. The men would disappear into the moving truck, parked halfway on the sidewalk, and reappear with some small part of Sol and Connie's life. Their father's night table was coming out as they left.

When the two children passed the first house next to their new home, a dog bounded out of the house with something in its mouth. The screen door must have been open. The dog was chocolate brown, smallish, with long hair and floppy ears. It ran fast. Sol and Connie didn't have a chance to move before it was upon them. Luckily it was a friendly dog. It ran circles around them, wagging its tail and barking from the throat, while at the same time trying to keep whatever it had in its mouth from falling. This turned out to be a bone.

A woman walked out of the house—Fay Holaderry, the witch of this story. She was wrapped in a too-big dress that she held up at one shoulder as she crossed the lawn, so that she looked a little like a girl playing dress-up.

"Swift! Swift!" she called to the dog. "Leave the children alone." She came up to them. "I'm sorry about my dog. He got out somehow."

"It's okay, we love dogs," Connie said.

"Yes, but still he shouldn't do that. Down, Swift," she called.

The dog had started jumping up with its front paws on Sol. Sol played with him by pulling on the bone in a tug-of-war. Swift took this very seriously. He dug his paws in and pulled back, growling, but in a friendly way.

"That one loves his lunch." Holaderry laughed. Then she looked at the sister and brother. "But I don't think I've seen you two around here before."

"We're just moving in today," Connie said.

Holaderry glanced at the truck parked up on the sidewalk. "Oh yes, I see. I've been indoors all morning." A smile spread across her face. "You have a big family?"

"Just us and our parents," Sol answered, glancing up while still playing tug-of-war with the dog. He tugged on the bone. The dog tugged back. Sometime during this game, a puzzled expression crept onto Sol's face. There was something strange about that bone.

"Well, let me be the first to welcome you to the neighborhood," the woman said, holding out her hand. "My name's Fay. Fay Holaderry. And this is my dog, Swift."

Sol let go of the bone, wiped his hands on his pants, and shook Holaderry's hand. Connie shook Holaderry's hand too, looking into the woman's eyes as she did. She could usually tell a lot from a person's eyes. But Holaderry's were shut like a gate, so Connie could only see what was on the outside of the woman. Bright tomato red hair. Crow's-feet wrinkles at the corners of her eyes.

"It's so nice to have kids around," Holaderry went on. "There are none left on this block. They've all . . . they've all gone." She glanced at the apartment building as if she could see through it into their new home. She smiled. "I'll have to have you over for dinner, one of these days."

"That's very nice of you, Mrs. Holaderry, thanks for the invitation," Sol said politely. "Come on, Connie, let's go to the park. It's been nice to meet you," he said to the woman.

Holaderry glanced curiously at Sol. "Yes, very nice to meet you too," she said. "Swift and I should get back to what we were doing. Come on, Swift boy."

Connie scratched Swift on the head. "Goodbye, Swift," she said. "Goodbye," she said to Holaderry.

As they walked down the block, past driveways and gardens, Sol asked, "Did you notice anything strange about that woman, Connie?"

"I think so. There *was* something strange."

Sol felt as if Holaderry was still watching them. But when he looked back, no one was there.

No one, that is, but a wood thrush that eyed them carefully from the grass, then took off and flew over an eave in the direction of the town center. That thrush had gone to report on Sol and Connie's arrival. You see, Holaderry wasn't the only woman from the old forest who had stayed after the trees had been cut down. Another had stayed, and she was of a different kind, the woman with this thrush.

But Sol didn't pay any attention to the bird. He turned and saw, across the street, a low building with double doors. A sign in front read GRAND CREEK LIBRARY. Steps led to the main entrance.

"How about we go in there," he said to Connie, "just for a little while. There's something I want to look up."

"I thought we were going to the park, like normal kids."

"I *am* normal," Sol said. And, to prove his point, he did exactly what Connie wanted. He went with her to the park.

It looked like any town park, a lawn of

summer-dry grass, a path offering benches for the occasional walker to sit on. Except that, far in the distance over the houses of the town, mountains loomed. Sol and Connie weren't used to seeing mountains from their home. In fact, they had never seen mountains like that in real life at all.

"They look so close," Connie said. "Do you think we could walk there?"

"They're much farther than they look," Sol answered. "You'd have to drive a long time to reach them."

Sol and Connie spent more than an hour in the park, throwing the ball and the Frisbee. The air was heavy with humidity. When Connie threw the Frisbee, it glided straight and slow through that air, right to Sol. But Sol could never throw a Frisbee straight. When he threw it, it tilted, shot off to the side, and landed on its edge, rolling like a wheel across the grass.

A couple of years ago, if he'd thrown a Frisbee wrong like that while playing with other kids, he would have immediately launched into an explanation of *how* a Frisbee flew. He'd talk about air pressure and the shape of a Frisbee's edges. By explaining how it flew, Sol showed that he knew something the others didn't, even if he was a lousy thrower.

But at age eleven he'd outgrown having to prove himself to other kids. He knew it wasn't important if he could throw a Frisbee straight. He couldn't be good at everything. That was life.

Connie chased after the Frisbee as it rolled away. She grabbed it, ran back, swung her arm forward, and the Frisbee took flight, gliding perfectly to him.

That was the way a Frisbee should fly.

"Let's throw the ball," Sol said. They were both good at that. So they switched to the ball and threw it back and forth, thoroughly enjoying themselves—for the first and last time in Grand Creek—as the sun dipped behind the mountains and a breeze rose.

When they finished and were headed back, Sol said, "Let's go to the library now. There's something I want to check." He crossed the street and walked up the library steps. Connie stayed close behind.

Sol had a new mission that afternoon, forming

in his mind since they'd left their neighbor and her dog. He wanted to find out exactly what kind of bone the dog had been playing with. There was something strange about it, that much he was sure of. Sol knew a lot about the anatomy of animals. Most dog bones came from cows, he thought, or maybe also sheep. If that bone had been a cow or sheep bone, though, something was totally wrong about its size and shape.

Inside the library, the computers in the children's section had a sign on them: TEMPORARILY DOWN.

Sol told Connie, "I'll meet you here in a minute."

He walked to the main Internet computers, but they were all being used. Checking the sign-in list, he saw it would be more than an hour before he could get online. So he went to the catalog computer instead to search for books on the library shelves.

Sol typed in *animal anatomy*, his fingers tap-tapping on the keyboard. Books came up with names like *Bovine Anatomy* and *Guide to Animal Anatomy and Physiology*.

He went into the stacks to find those and similar ones. Most of the books he pulled off the shelf were too complicated even for many adults, but Sol wasn't daunted. One book on display with a bright blue cover caught his eye. *Human Anatomy*. He took that one too.

He carried everything to a table in the children's section and quickly grew absorbed in his books.

Connie, meanwhile, was wandering the aisles and starting to amuse herself with a new game. She crouched hidden in one aisle and peered over the books on the shelf into the next aisle. Then she reached in carefully and pushed books facing that aisle off the shelf. For someone in that aisle, those books fell off very mysteriously.

A small boy walking there saw two books fall out, on their own, next to him. *He* hadn't touched them. He turned and walked the other way, but books flew off the shelf near wherever he stood. He ran away to his mother, frightened.

Connie was readying to target her next victim when a librarian appeared behind her. Connie jumped.

"I'm going to have to ask you to behave, young lady," the librarian said. She had a square jaw, bright rosy cheeks, and an all-knowing look in her eyes. "Now, can I help you find a book?"

"Sure." Connie put a finger to her chin, rather like her brother did when he was thinking. "*War and Peace*," she said.

The librarian did not look amused. "I'm afraid that book might not be right for you."

"Are you saying I'm dumb?" Connie challenged the librarian.

"No. It's just that Tolstoy goes on and on about history and the individual's place in history. It does get a bit tiresome."

"Okay, then. *Wuthering Heights*."

The woman studied Connie. "What are you doing in the library on such a beautiful day?"

"My brother and I just moved here, and he wanted to look stuff up." She pointed at Sol, who was sitting at the table in the children's section, a stack of books in front of him.

"Where?" The librarian looked at Sol's table, but she must not have realized Connie meant Sol, because, with his long hair below his shoulders, he looked for all the world like a girl.

Connie hated when people made that mistake. "Over there," she said. "The *boy* with the *long hair*."

"Oh, I see," the librarian said. "Well, you'd better stay with him, then." She walked off quickly, looking glad to leave Connie behind.

Connie joined Sol at the table. "Have you found what you're looking for?"

Sol was staring intently at one page in the blue book. It was labeled FEMUR BONE.

He looked up distractedly. "Hmm? Oh yeah. I guess so. I guess so," he repeated. He closed the heavy book. "Come on, let's go."

A BET LOST, A CAT GONE

WHEN THEY GOT HOME the movers had gone. Sol and Connie were officially moved into their new home. The apartment was strewn with boxes rising in makeshift towers. Mr. and Mrs. Blink, standing in the midst of those boxes, looked as if Sol and Connie had interrupted them during an important conversation. They stopped talking, but kept giving each other looks.

They were just the type of father and stepmother that you'd expect to find in a story like this, except that Mr. Blink had a secret.

Sol remembered his bet with Connie right away and went into the kitchen to check the glass of ice water, sure that the ice would have melted and he'd have won. Connie followed him.

Sol stopped short when he got to the glass.

"I guess I lost the bet, huh?" Connie said.

After a long, confused pause, Sol said, "No. You were right. The water *is* a little higher."

"I'm right?" Connie sounded surprised. "I won three bucks? Great! Hand it over."

Sol fished three dollars out of his pocket. He handed the money to her. Then he studied the glass intently, peering at the tape mark. He put his eye right up to it.

"But it's impossible," he said, although he didn't sound so certain anymore. "Scientifically impossible."

"Maybe the ice is different from what you're used to," Connie said. "Or maybe you don't know science as well as you . . ." but she stopped before finishing that sentence. It was obvious from Sol's grimace that his mind had gone back to The

Terrible Day from last spring, the day of their old school's science fair.

"It doesn't matter," Connie said more sympathetically, pocketing her winnings. "Let's go unpack. I need your help."

When they stepped into the living room, Mr. Blink was talking quietly again with Mrs. Blink, and opening a box, which made a loud scraping sound that filled the room. He stopped talking at once, though, and turned to Sol and Connie, smiling.

"I meant to tell you, Connie," he said, trying to sound cheerful, "I decided not to ship your bed. There simply wasn't space in the truck. Until we order you a new bed, which we're sure to do, I thought you could share your brother's bunk bed."

"Share a room?" Connie immediately complained, and Sol joined his voice to hers.

Mrs. Blink interrupted. "Consider yourselves lucky," she said, laughing. "Things could be worse."

This comment of Mrs. Blink's, looked at in a certain light, might be understood as the positive view of an optimist.

But Connie only heard it and wondered: How much worse could things be?

Connie was thinking of her cat, who, like the bed, hadn't come with them.

Quantum.

He was the family's cat, but really he'd been Connie's cat. At least that's how Connie saw it. Only, Sol had named him, for a scientific theory, of course.

Connie had loved Quantum very much. He was a beautiful black cat. He could leap from the floor to the kitchen counter to the top of the kitchen cabinets in one quick move. Or he lazed on Mr. Blink's favorite chair when Mr. Blink wasn't around. Then, Connie would stroke him, pick him up, and send him over to Sol.

"Be nice," she'd tell Quantum. "He's your brother." Quantum would pad over to Sol and, as if he were doing Sol a favor, let Sol pet him.

Quantum treated most humans as if they were beneath him. His look, while he licked his paws, seemed to say, "You *wish* you could be like me. But, I'm sorry, it simply isn't possible."

Except he never looked that way at Connie. He came to her whenever she wanted him to. She stroked his soft fur and felt him purring under her palm. Connie loved it that Quantum had picked her and ignored everybody else, because she felt that animals understood her in a way that people never did. She thought it was amazing how you could look an animal in the eyes and see the animal thinking and feeling just like a person.

Mr. Blink had never liked Quantum, though.

"More work for me, isn't he?" he'd said. "Cats need to eat. And they poop and pee in that little box." Mr. Blink made a face. "You'd better do everything for him if you want to keep him, or your brother had better do it. Or the cat's gone."

Connie had kept her end of the bargain, taking good care of Quantum. But then Mrs. Blink had come along, and, suddenly, the deal was off.

"I can't stand cats," she announced in front of the whole family. Noting Connie's expression, something between anger and tears, she changed her tactic. Her face softened and she smiled sadly. "I'm allergic to cats, you see." She faked a sneeze.

Connie wasn't fooled. "They make me itch." She started scratching all over. "The cat will have to go, honey," she said to Mr. Blink.

"A good idea," Mr. Blink agreed.

Connie did everything she could to keep Quantum, but in the end she failed. Quantum had to go. Luckily, Connie was able to place Quantum with her friend Ruth, whose family had a small farm and two cats and two dogs already. Connie saw Quantum over there every week, where he had quickly established himself as king of the dogs while ignoring the other cats. Quantum seemed to enjoy his new home. That made Connie feel a little better.

And Connie understood that you couldn't always keep a pet.

Still, she'd said to Sol later, "Look, Sol, I don't have anything against stepmoms. I know that a stepmom might *really* be allergic to cats. I know a stepmom could even hate cats and still be okay in the end—"

"Exactly," Sol said. "When someone new shows up, it takes time, and there are always problems

along the way. Kids face those problems, though."
Sol nodded, absorbed in making his point. "And
they make it through and end up getting along well
with stepparents. Even though it may seem really
hard at the beginning."

"But," Connie went on, "Quantum's gone. . . .
What's next?"

Sol pushed his hair back out of his eyes. "We'll
just have to wait and see," he said, always reason-
able.

Very soon after, the four of them had moved to
Grand Creek.

SECRET CONVERSATIONS

AT THE END of that first day, Sol's bedroom was partly ready for him and Connie. His bunk bed, dresser, and night table were set up. Sol and Connie had taken out their favorite books and games. But there were still boxes everywhere in the bedroom. When it came time to sleep, Sol took the top bunk and Connie the bottom.

Mr. Blink checked to make sure they were in bed. He told them that they'd be going into town the next day, and closed the door.

After a while, lying in the dark, Connie whispered, "You're not going to fall on me, are you?"

"No," Sol called down, "I'm not going to fall on you."

"Because every time you move, the bed just

shakes and shakes. I don't think it's strong enough to hold you up."

"It's plenty strong, Connie. That's what it's made for."

"That's easy for you to say. You aren't lying right under a bed. If you fall, I'd be crushed in an instant. Squish, just like that. Just like a bug—"

"I'm not going to fall on you!" Sol said. "Now go to sleep."

There was a pause. "Maybe it's better if I slept on top."

"All right, tomorrow you can sleep on top."

Connie hesitated, as if deciding whether that was good enough.

"Okay," she said finally. "Okay, fine. Tomorrow."

"Good night, Connie."

"Good night."

WITH Sol and Connie in bed, Mr. and Mrs. Blink talked quietly in their own bedroom. You might be expecting this conversation, since you almost certainly know the story of another father and stepmother, from long ago, in a similar situation. And, as has already been mentioned, Mr. and Mrs. Blink were very much like those two. Except that Mr. Blink had a secret.

And his secret was this: He wasn't actually himself. Well, he was himself, of course, but he wasn't Mr. Blink. Well, he *was* Mr. Blink, but he wasn't Sol and Connie's father. He was Sol and Connie's father's identical twin brother. He was *the other* Mr. Blink.

Long ago, just after Sol and Connie's mother had fallen off the ice shelf—an early casualty of

global warming—the original Mr. Blink had gone to check on the accident and see the dwindling South Pole for himself, leaving Sol and Connie with an aunt. And then Mr. Blink, Sol and Connie's father, had disappeared, but nobody knew it. Because his twin brother, Mr. Blink, came back in his place.

Connie was only a baby at the time, so, if she noticed, she was unable to say anything to anyone. Sol was three and did notice something had changed, but at three all the world is new, and Sol had to watch everyone else to decide whether something was normal or not. And no one else realized that anything extraordinary had happened. Mr. Blink looked exactly the same, he sounded the same, he even smelled the same, using all the same soaps. He did come back acting a little differently, but that was easy to understand given the circumstances of his trip.

Nobody knew, of course, that Sol and Connie's father was going to inherit a stake in a very important company, the Silicon Hyperspace Allied Manufacturers Company, from an aging uncle. Even Sol and Connie's father hadn't known. But the *other* Mr. Blink had heard it from an insider at the company who knew the uncle well. And he also found out that he himself would inherit nothing. So he'd arranged to get rid of his twin brother—in the southern lands where flamingos stood in lonely deep blue pools amid the wild grasses—and then replaced him, sure that he wouldn't have to wait long for the inheritance.

But the aging uncle had kept aging, with no end in sight.

To tell the truth, Mr. Blink wasn't all that surprised. He often judged wrong. Although he was still sure his luck would turn one day and he'd finally be proven right—either about everything, or about some things, or at least about a few things, once in a while. I have to be right sometime, he thought.

Meanwhile, Sol and Connie were growing up. They got used to Mr. Blink, accepted his distant manners, believed him to be their father, and forgot any strange events from their early childhood.

Then Mr. Blink had married, and the woman he married, who became the new Mrs. Blink, was rotten to the core.

———

ROTTENNESS runs in certain families. Mrs. Blink had long ago traced her family history and discovered that she was related to many important rotten people from the past. One of them was a famous queen who had said, "Let them eat cake!" which doesn't sound very rotten, but actually was. Another was a queen who passed out poison apples, and yet another was the famous stepmother from the old story about the witch who ate children. (If you must know exactly how they were related, Mrs. Blink was the eleventh cousin, fifteen times removed, of that older stepmother.)

So many rotten ancestors, thought Mrs. Blink happily. She was proud to come from a line of such un-greatness.

When she married Mr. Blink, she immediately traced his family history too, and discovered, to her wonder and delight, that Mr. Blink himself had rotten ancestors. And one of them was the father from the very same tale about the witch. (Mr. Blink was the seventh cousin, twelve times removed, of that more ancient father, and this, actually, was true even though Mr. Blink was pretending to be his brother, which Mrs. Blink didn't know.)

As soon as she found out, Mrs. Blink told Mr. Blink all about the rotten roots of their family trees.

"It can't be an accident that we're related to that couple from the famous story," she said. "It was meant to be." She pointed to their ancestors then, and suggested, in her most persuasive voice, that they should continue the family tradition and get rid of the children. Because wasn't that what was wrong with people today, she said, that they weren't traditional enough?

"I don't know," Mr. Blink had replied. "Some traditions seem better than others."

Still, privately, he wondered about it. It *was* strange that they were descendants of that older couple. Could it be destiny?

And after several more talks on the same subject, Mr. Blink started saying things that showed he was slowly coming to agree with his wife.

"Have you ever noticed," he said, "that exactly when I need the bathroom really badly, one of them is always using it and I have to wait for what seems like forever? That's not so easy, holding it in, you know."

And later, he asked Mrs. Blink, "We'd have

more room in the house, then, wouldn't we? For a Ping-Pong table?"

But the clincher was when he received an email—the first in years—from the insider who knew his still-aging uncle at Silicon Hyperspace Allied Manufacturers. The email read: "The inheritance will skip a generation if there are children. Repeat, inheritance all goes to the children, if there are any." Mr. Blink had to read this email several times before he fully understood. It was hard to grasp the legal jargon. He wasn't a lawyer, after all.

But finally he got it, and then he went to Mrs. Blink and said, "I was thinking about . . . what you told me. Before. And, you know, I always wanted to go on vacation, to the south part of the world. I was . . . there once. But we don't have the money. Unless . . ."

"Unless what?" Mrs. Blink asked, pretending not to understand her husband.

"Unless we did what you suggested earlier."

"Did I suggest that . . . thing you're talking about?" Mrs. Blink asked. "Are you sure it wasn't you who said it?"

"Well, I guess it doesn't really matter who said it first," Mr. Blink admitted, although privately he thought that it definitely had been Mrs. Blink. But then, he knew what she was saying. It didn't make him any less rotten, that she'd said it first. He'd known all along, of course, that he was rotten—like his new wife, and not like his brother.

Mr. Blink took over the research from Mrs. Blink afterward, to find out where their ancestors—the other father and stepmother from that older story—had lived. Mr. Blink was determined to show, at least, that he wasn't as dumb as he privately suspected he was. And, amazingly, he did it. He tracked the witch to Grand Creek, and they'd moved.

Tonight's discussion in the new house, then, was just the latest of many. Tonight, they discussed the plan itself. Mr. and Mrs. Blink's voices drifted from their bedroom into the hallway, but not as far as the kids' bedroom.

"Did you find out where she lives, exactly?" Mrs. Blink asked.

"Nobody knows. She keeps it a secret. She has

some sort of system. But don't worry, I've got it all figured out."

"Are you sure?"

"Do you doubt your husband?"

"Uh . . . well . . ."

"All I've got to do," Mr. Blink continued, "is take them into town on a Tuesday and leave them near a certain spot. And that's tomorrow. Simple as that. The w—" He stopped. "She does the rest."

His voice fell silent. He went to the bedroom door and opened it. He stepped out in his pajamas— which had giraffes on them—and peered up and down the hall. Satisfied that no one was there, he stepped back into the bedroom.

After Mr. and Mrs. Blink's bedroom door shut, Sol came out of the bathroom. He'd needed an extra bathroom trip. All he had heard as he'd crossed the hallway were his father's last words: *Near a certain spot, and that's tomorrow, simple as that, the w—, she does the rest*. It wasn't anything truly suspicious. But there was something in his father's tone that Sol didn't like.

THE TERRIBLE DAY

Tuesday

SOL HAD TROUBLE sleeping. He got up very early, when it was still night, climbing down without waking Connie. She lay asleep, breathing shallowly, a shadowy form on the lower bunk.

Sol looked out the window at Holaderry's house. There, a single light shone softly behind a closed curtain on the second floor. Dark vines climbed a trellis beside the window.

Sol thought about what he'd learned that day in the library, but became distracted when, glancing at his homemade clock-and-weather device on the windowsill, he noticed it read: "**64°, 859 MB, 3:49AM,**" and "**SUNNY.**"

He looked out the window again. It wasn't

sunny, it was nighttime. The weather prediction was wrong, he realized, because he hadn't programmed the device to check the time of day when it guessed the weather. He should have programmed it to read "CLEAR" at night, for the same weather conditions that made it "SUNNY" during the day.

Why couldn't he have thought of that, he wondered. It was such a simple mistake.

Sol had so many things on his mind that he wasn't sure what was keeping him awake. Was it his bet with Connie, which he still couldn't explain? Was it what he'd learned from his research in the library? The conversation he'd overheard that evening? Or maybe it was just things from the past that were in his mind right then.

The town he'd grown up in.

His school.

The Terrible Day.

Last spring, after it was all over, a group of boys who were definitely not his friends had invited him to come with them after school, and for some reason he'd said yes. As if things between them had suddenly changed. The group who called Sol the "bad scientist," a nickname that had developed from an earlier one, the "mad scientist."

During the walk one boy had whispered in another's ear, obviously about Sol, and both had laughed. Then the other boys said, "Tell us, tell us," and the first boy whispered in their ears, but not Sol's, and everyone laughed except Sol. They arrived at one of the boys' houses and he said to Sol, "We'll just be a few minutes, okay?"

"Okay," Sol answered.

Sol had waited outside for five minutes. Ten minutes. Twenty minutes. Whenever anyone passed by, he pretended to be looking at a very fascinating weed growing on the sidewalk. Until, finally, he'd gone home.

It had all happened because of The Terrible Day, the school science fair day. Sol had decided to build something very special for the fair that year, something that would prove how smart he was: a heat detection device that could measure heat patterns from a distance of up to seventy-two yards. He'd wanted to surprise everyone, even Connie, so he worked in private, his bedroom door jammed shut from the inside. When he wasn't working, he put a padlock on his closet, where he stored all of his stuff.

Seeing how he was acting, Connie declared that she wouldn't let Sol see her science fair entry either. She made a big show of closing her bedroom door when she worked on it. She told Sol, "Don't come in, or you'll get it."

"As if I care," Sol said. "What are you going to do on your own?"

But despite his harsh words, Sol privately worried about Connie, because his little sister wasn't any good in science and he'd always helped her on things like this before. He knew she wasn't really working on anything for the science fair when she closed her door.

Sol even considered letting Connie in on his

secret just so she'd let him help her on her entry. But this time his project was too special. He wanted to do it all on his own.

Sol's teacher, Ms. Alma, encouraged him. Although she didn't know at first what he was working on either—he kept it a secret even from her—she knew that it had to be good.

"Won't you love to win that scholarship, Sol?" she said. The winner of the science fair was going to receive a scholarship to a special camp with real scientists as teachers, near a high-tech invention called a particle accelerator. "To see the particle accelerator in action? I know you have a really great chance of winning."

On another day, Ms. Alma took Sol aside. "I'm sure you're working on something extra special. If you could tell me what it is, I might be able to arrange something special for you too. You see, the principal is thinking of having some of the best students do presentations for the whole school. So I told him, let's start with Sol, and he agreed, and we came up with a couple of other names too. But I need to know what you're building."

So Sol told her, with her promise that she would keep it a secret from everyone, even Principal Warrick if she could. She agreed and a few days later, she told him, "It's all arranged."

Ms. Alma had been a fantastic teacher. Sol loved her, to this day. Not in *that* way. Just because she'd understood him so well.

As the fair was fast approaching, Sol worked on the device in his bedroom, piecing together circuit boards and computer chips, his mind full with images of the day to come. He knew he should have cared about the invention for itself, not about winning or prizes. Winning didn't matter, he told himself. Scientists, he thought, did science for science's sake.

But Sol discovered that he did care about winning. During the weeks leading up to the fair, he saw the triumphant day to come everywhere around him. He sat down to eat cereal in the mornings with Connie, looked into his bowl and saw, strangely, the word *Success* written there—if he looked into the milk closely enough, that is, though the word disappeared right after that. And on the bus ride to school past the farms, he looked out the window at the gas station letter board sign that read OIL CHANGE, FRESH FARM EGGS, HAPPY EASTER, and saw, in his mind, the sign announcing SOL, CHILD GENIUS, WINS THE SCIENCE FAIR.

When Ms. Alma taught a lesson in class that he already knew, and he was bored, Sol imagined her standing in front of the class instead, shouting: "Sol, you won the scholarship!"

And the evening before the science fair, after Sol tested his heat detection device for the final time and locked it in his closet for safekeeping— where he was sure nothing could happen to it—he went outside to the backyard and peered through his telescope. Saturn was in the night sky. He could see Saturn's rings as a line across the planet, and he thought, if he had a strong enough telescope, he might even see the words SOL WINS written in the giant carbon-and-ice boulders of those rings.

Sol could have sworn then that someone was watching him. But when he turned to look behind, there was just his bedroom window—he'd left the light on—and his half-closed curtain.

On the day of the science fair, Sol and Connie took the bus to school, Sol with his big box and Connie with a backpack. Sol dragged his box through the main entrance, into Ms. Alma's classroom, and pushed it into a corner.

Once he was sure that the box was secure and not drawing any attention to itself, he went off to look at the rest of the exhibits. He noticed right away, as he watched kids from his grade setting up, that they'd brought the simplest of fair entries. No one had really done anything but make boards with information. The most popular boy in Sol's class had set up a worm farm. WORMS AND HOW THEY LIVE, said the poster. The only interesting fact on the poster was that worms had five hearts. Everybody knows that, thought Sol.

The smartest kid in the class besides Sol, a tall girl named Anna, had set up a table titled GENETICALLY ENGINEERED CROPS AND THE SPOILING OF THE GENE POOL. It was a brave thing for her to do because they lived in a farming region and all of the farmers used GE seeds. Many of the kids' parents were farmers, including, Sol was pretty sure,

Anna's own family. Sol decided that her entry was very good. Anna was one of the students who would be presenting, Ms. Alma had told him. But still, Sol thought, Anna's entry was only an informational presentation. It didn't work, like his.

Sol headed toward the other end of the school, where the younger kids were setting up, curious about Connie's entry. He wished that she had let him help her and was thinking this when he came upon Connie's table in the corridor. Sol saw that things were even worse than he had imagined.

Her so-called scientific experiment was titled MAGNETS ATTRACT!!!

On her table were two lonely magnets, stuck together. There was also one flat refrigerator magnet beside them, which, Sol was pretty sure, he'd seen on their own refrigerator just that morning. She'd probably thought of bringing it at the last minute.

"Hi, Connie," he said, trying to be cheerful. But he couldn't hide his disappointment.

"Hi, Sol," Connie said.

"It's a cool experiment," Sol said, pointing to the two magnets stuck together.

"Whatever."

"You know, you could also have done something on how magnets make electricity. I could still maybe find you a coil of wire, and an ammeter—"

"I don't need your help," Connie said. "I know you think it's lame. Don't worry about it. Have you checked your own invention?"

Connie seemed nervous, and looked very interested in the answer to this question.

"I tested it yesterday. It's all set to go."

"Maybe you should check it again."

"It's much too complicated to check quickly, Connie." Sol thought that she was trying to change the subject.

He glanced at the two feeble magnets on the table and the refrigerator magnet. "Really, I know where they keep the science equipment here. I could get you some extra magnet things. Iron filings—"

"It's okay!" Connie shouted.

"Maybe next year," Sol said. He was a little upset that Connie had apparently learned so little about science from him. She hadn't even put an explanation of poles on her sign. Or of magnetic fields. The poster, Sol saw, really should have said OPPOSITES ATTRACT!!! not MAGNETS ATTRACT!!!

Connie understood what Sol was thinking, just by looking at the expression on his face.

"I'm younger than you," she said. "Our science fair isn't like yours."

"Okay," he answered, giving up. "I just came by to remind you that my demonstration is going to be the first one, at ten exactly, on the big kids' field. So don't be late. You know, you *could* have written 'Opposites Attract,' because magnets have two poles, and—"

"I know, I just didn't want to," Connie said.

Sol didn't believe it.

Connie sighed. "Please go and check everything for your presentation."

"Wait till you see it," Sol said, smiling. "It's really something fantastic."

Connie looked even more nervous than ever. She turned her head away. "Good luck, Sol," she said.

At a quarter to ten, the secretary's voice

announced on the PA system that the school should come out to the big kids' field "to watch special demonstrations by our fifth-graders." Sol went back to the classroom when the announcement sounded. Ms. Alma helped him carry his box out to the field. Sol unloaded it, a flat black unit with legs that folded out, a small satellite dish pointing from the front, and a large computer screen with input-output ports.

He aimed it at the school.

Anna was there with her informational boards on genetic engineering, and two students from the other fifth-grade class were there with their own presentations—one on heat and air pressure, the other on the strength of arches. The classes were already assembling, falling into rows that the teachers organized. The kids were messing around and weren't really paying attention to Sol. The school principal arrived. Then everyone quieted down.

Sol positioned the big screen so that all of the students could see its display. He looked out at the mass of students and teachers before him. He was glad to see that Connie had arrived at the front of her class and gotten a good spot. She was halfway back on the far left side.

Sol checked his watch. It was ten o'clock.

It was all just as he had imagined it. Almost. The principal delivered a short speech, after scolding a group of fourth-graders who were loudly misbehaving. He talked of his expectation that they would "see some truly fascinating science." Sol fidgeted, growing nervous. A couple of kids shouted out something about the "mad scientist."

Sol thought about how much his life would change after this. Already, he told himself, standing up in front of everyone with the principal beside him, it had started to change for the better.

After the principal's introduction, Sol stepped up. He looked at Ms. Alma. He said as loudly as he could, "My science fair entry is a long-distance heat detection device."

Ms. Alma gestured to show him to look at the whole school.

Sol turned and looked out at the kids. "My science fair entry is a long-distance heat detection

device," he repeated. "I built it myself from spare parts. Some devices like this already exist, but mine has special features. It not only shows the heat in its range, but it also tells what things could be making the heat that it detects. A wildfire, say, or hot lamps, electric heaters, a large number of people together, even sunlight. It does this by measuring the parameters of the heat and making an educated guess based on that information." Sol didn't know if the kids understood him or not. "The screen displays this guess on the right-hand side. Now I'd like to demonstrate it on the school."

He switched his invention on.

He felt a painful shock course through his body as he flicked the switch. He was thrown to the ground by its force. Looking up, he saw the device spark. A tiny puff of smoke arose.

The screen started flashing things he had typed in during his early tests.

"Connie can be annoying," the screen flashed.

"I am a genius," the screen flashed.

"I love Ms. Alma."

"Principal Warrick is dumb."

All of the students roared with laughter. Or

maybe that was the roar in Sol's head from the electric shock.

Ms. Alma stood frozen in her spot, hesitating a second too long before she approached Sol.

The principal didn't laugh when his own name showed up.

Then someone shouted, "The school's on fire!"

A cloud of smoke had appeared from the cafeteria window inside the school.

Sol jumped to his feet. The students were a blur through his tears. He realized he was crying. His presentation was nothing like he had imagined it.

He turned and ran. He sprinted off the school grounds.

He ran down the block.

He ran all the way home.

He ran into his house and into his bedroom. He threw himself on the bed.

What had he done wrong? He kicked his mattress and hit his pillow. The device should have worked. But it hadn't. Then he thought: Had someone said the school was on fire?

He would never go to that summer camp or

study with brilliant scientists. He would never see the particle accelerator. He would never go anywhere.

He wasn't sure that he could even return to school.

Connie came home later. "Don't worry, they stopped the fire quickly," she said. "The kids are split on whether it was your heat invention or just the cafeteria cook. Only a few things were ruined. And one cafeteria wall got burned. It looks like some kind of black monster on the wall."

She handed over the box that he'd kept the device in. Connie had put his stuff back into it, jumbled up. She looked very sad.

Sol never did find out what had gone wrong. He began taking it apart later that night, looking for miswiring, but gave up before he finished. He didn't have the strength. He put it back in the box, half-assembled, and shoved it into his closet, which he no longer bothered to lock.

Connie, meanwhile, had gotten a green star for her magnet project, which was pretty much what all of the kids her age got.

"You can build your device again," she said to Sol. "Why not? It was probably just a little thing. You'll win a scholarship another year."

Connie was intent on cheering him up. She even went out and bought him a present. She handed it to him sheepishly. It was a plaque with a famous quote from Thomas Edison.

It read: MANY OF LIFE'S FAILURES ARE PEOPLE WHO DID NOT REALIZE HOW CLOSE THEY WERE TO SUCCESS WHEN THEY GAVE UP.

"Is this supposed to make me feel better?" Sol asked. "I know I'm a failure. You don't have to remind me."

"Sol," Connie had said, "you're not a failure."

NOW, Sol sat in the darkness of the bedroom. His clock-and-weather device read, "63°, 859 MB, 4:41AM," and "SUNNY."

He looked at Connie asleep, her face in shadow, quiet breathing sounds coming out of her mouth—the only sounds in the room. He glanced at the closet door. Why had he brought the failed invention with him, he wondered. It was time to get rid of it once and for all.

He stood and stretched, pushing his hair back, and peered out the window. The light in Holaderry's house had gone off.

They had other problems now.

Sol wondered whether he should tell Connie what he'd learned from the book in the library, or if she'd be better off not knowing.

CONNIE was surprised to find her brother up when she awoke. It was very early, judging by the soft light that streamed into the room. Sol looked tired.

"What's wrong?" she asked.

He gazed at her, his thin lips pressed together as they did whenever he had a mystery to solve. "Connie, listen, that bone that the dog had yesterday," he said, "it was a human bone."

6

CARING FOR ALL CREATURES, BIG AND SMALL

THE SUN ROSE in Grand Creek that Tuesday morning, lighting the mountains. Wood thrushes chattered in short cries outside Sol and Connie's bedroom window.

Their calls drifted in, where Sol sat on the edge of the lower bunk. He'd made a list of all the reasons the woman's dog might have been chewing on a human bone. Making a list was the logical approach. They could consider all the possibilities and narrow them down after.

He explained this to Connie, who was sitting up in bed.

"Want to hear the list?" Sol asked.

Connie nodded.

"First, she could be a doctor," Sol said.

"Why would she have that bone, then?"

"It could be from one of those model skeletons," Sol explained. "They use real bones for those. Or maybe she amputated a leg once."

"At home? And kept the bone for a souvenir?"

Sol shrugged. "We have to consider all the possibilities. Next," he read off the list, "she's an undertaker."

"What's that?"

"You know, someone who does funerals."

"Isn't she supposed to *bury* the bodies?"

"Maybe it was from a body she's working on right now."

"It wasn't a whole leg, just the bone."

"Whatever. It's still possible." Sol seemed to be getting upset. He cleared his throat. "Okay, this is the last one I've got so far. She's a scientist. She does experiments on bone transplants or something like that, and it was from her research laboratory."

"That's a good one."

"You like that? Good." He starred it on the list. "Okay, can you think of any more?"

Connie thought about it.

"Not really," she said.

"I'm sure there must be others. But we'll start with these. If she's a doctor, she should be registered with the state. An undertaker also has to register, I think, and she would have a business listing too. If she's a scientist, we can probably find her online at some university, or at least some of her papers." Sol bit his pencil. "It's too bad we don't have the Internet set up here yet. We'll have to look it up at the library. I can't think of any other way to get information on her. Not really," he added.

They went out to the kitchen for breakfast. Mr. and Mrs. Blink were already drinking coffee and eating eggs. When Mr. Blink saw them, he smiled and—as part of what he thought of as his brilliant plan to mislead them—took out his phone and made a call. He watched the children the whole time to make sure they were paying attention.

"Yes, hello," he said into the phone, "this is Mr.

Blink here. I called before about getting a babysitter for tomorrow. Wednesday. Yes. So expensive? Well, it doesn't matter, my kids are worth it."

He finished making the arrangements, hung up, and nodded at Sol and Connie. "See?" he said. "Everything's perfectly normal. Today is Tuesday and we'll be going into town. There's nothing strange about that. And since you will definitely still be here tomorrow"—he coughed—"we need that babysitter, no matter what the cost."

"Have fun, dear," Mrs. Blink said. "Goodbye," she said to Sol and Connie.

Mr. Blink grinned, pushed his chair back with a screech, and, stepping over an unpacked box, picked up his keys from the counter. They clinked as he put them in his pocket.

"Let's go."

"I'll just be a second," Sol said. He hurried back to his bedroom and came out pushing folded papers into his back pocket. "Ready," he said.

Behind the apartment building was a parking lot with eight spots. Sol, Connie, and Mr. Blink got into their car and pulled out of the lot. They turned right, so that they drove by Holaderry's house. A short man with a strangely small head came from the house, whistling. He wore a T-shirt that said LACAVILLA CAMP. He spotted Sol and Connie driving by and staring at him through the car window. He quickly turned and ran the other way.

"We could ask that guy about her," Connie said to Sol, half-joking.

"It didn't look like he wanted to talk to us," Sol said.

Sol watched the house until it disappeared from view behind them. What was in there, he wondered.

Mr. Blink drove them through the outskirts of town. Sol and Connie looked out the windows with great curiosity. They were used to farmland, and Grand Creek couldn't have been more different. Everything about the houses there seemed to defy the elements. Shutters hanging outside many windows could be closed against storms. The roofs were extremely steep, as if in imitation of the mountains in the distance, but they were made that way simply so the snow slid off in winter. And for protection against the summer sun, shade trees were planted in front.

It was a town built to withstand the tough weather of every season, a rugged town. On the other hand, there was cheer too. Expansive gardens grew in almost every yard. Metal and wood decorations were nailed to the fronts of houses, in the shapes of woodpeckers, butterflies, and other natural images. Many houses were painted in bright colors—red and white like a toadstool, or yellow, white, and green like a sunflower. Despite these small oddities, though, Grand Creek seemed to Sol and Connie like a normal town.

Long ago, other children had been led into the woods there, and those woods had looked normal too.

The truth is, you see, that one never can tell much from outward appearances.

Mr. Blink, meanwhile, was acting a bit strange that morning. He drove across a small bridge over a stream, then kept turning as if looking for somewhere in particular. And once he mumbled to himself, "That's the way the cookie crumbles."

"What, Dad?" Sol asked.

"Did I say something?"

"You said, 'That's the way the cookie crumbles.'"

"That's a weird thing to say," Mr. Blink had to admit.

He made a few more turns and finally parked on a lane of quiet houses. As they got out of the car, he said, "I've got some errands to run."

He led them to a cross street where there was a row of small shops. It wasn't the main street of Grand Creek, just a quiet road in one corner of the larger town.

At the corner, Sol said, "Oak."

"Huh?" Mr. Blink didn't understand.

"Oak Lane." Sol gestured toward the street sign. "That's where we're parked."

"Oh." Mr. Blink sounded as if he didn't like how much attention Sol paid to things. "I'll meet you back here in an hour," he said. "Or it might be . . . a little longer than that. You two walk around and enjoy yourselves." Mr. Blink headed quickly away from them and turned onto a side street.

They didn't know it, but Sol and Connie were lucky that they themselves chose to go left at that corner, and not right. They walked along the street of shops. Trees on both sides cast a web of shadows through which they crossed. A curio shop had an antique violin for sale in the window. An old grocery store had bins of apples and peaches out front. Sol and Connie went in. Sol bought an apple and Connie some Zigley's chewing gum from the old, hard-of-hearing man behind the counter, who had a fishing pole beside him. Coming out, they continued down the road to a shop behind a tree full of thrushes chattering nonstop.

Above the shop hung an old sign: ALL CREATURES, BIG AND SMALL. Square panes of glass, framed by thin wood strips, gave a view into the shop, which looked small and cluttered. A sheet taped up on the inside of one pane said DOG GROOMING AND CARE. EVERYTHING FOR CATS. CARING FOR ALL CREATURES, BIG AND SMALL.

In another pane was a flyer: ANSWER 3 RIDDLES AND WIN A PRIZE.

Sol paused in front of the flyer.

"You're good at riddles," Connie said. "Come on, let's go in and you can try them."

"I don't know. I couldn't even win our bet yesterday."

Connie turned away. She felt bad that he said that. She couldn't look him in the eyes. "Come on, Sol. Besides, I want to see the animals, if there are any."

She held the door open for him and they went in. Immediately they were struck by the smell of wet dog. Small rows of shelves held pet food, dog treats and collars, bird seed, colorful birdhouses, and empty glass aquariums. A big sheepdog stood in a raised bathtub near the back, being scrubbed by a man who looked so much like the dog that he must have been the dog's owner.

The shop manager, meanwhile, came out of a back room. A big woman, tall as a bear, she walked with a cane.

This woman really did care for all creatures, big and small, just as her sign said. She had been doing so for centuries. Like Holaderry, she'd lived in the shadow of the mountains for countless generations, before the town had been built. All then had been dense woodlands, bubbling brooks, and the air full of the sounds of insects, birds, and forest life. This woman had helped children escape from Holaderry if she found them in the forest first, or when the animals that she cared for found them.

But one night she and Holaderry had met during a terrible thunderstorm, and Holaderry had gotten the best of her. The witch stole from her a thing of great importance, and since that time she had lived under a curse. She couldn't help children out of the forest anymore, although she could still care for other creatures. When the town built up around them, she had started her shop—while Holaderry modernized her own house. She'd settled down and worked with all the animals and pets in Grand Creek, even Holaderry's dog, Swift.

Receiving word of Sol and Connie's arrival from a wood thrush, she still had hopes of helping them somehow. Although she hadn't worked out what she could do, right up to the moment when they walked into her shop.

The woman stepped up slowly to the children now and greeted them with a rhyme in a strange language, for she spoke many languages:

> *Drei Rätsel habe ich*
> *ihr lieben Kinderlein,*
> *werden euch sehr hilfreich sein.*

"German," Sol said quietly to Connie.

"What does it mean?"

"How should I know?"

She spoke again, in English. "Welcome, children," she said. "I was hoping you'd come into my shop. Here, I love all creatures—"

"Big and small," Connie said.

The manager pointed her cane at Connie. "I see you can read." She laughed. "Well, but I'm guessing—" Here she stared into Connie's eyes, and instead of Connie being able to judge the woman from the woman's eyes, Connie had the feeling that the manager herself could tell things about Connie. "I think that you love animals too," the manager said.

Connie nodded. For once she was a little quieter than usual, because there was something about this woman that she liked a lot, and that made her shy.

"Now, how can I help you?" the manager asked, thinking to herself: Unfortunately, not very much, I'm afraid.

"I was interested in the riddles," Sol said. "The three riddles? And then you win a prize?"

"I thought so. Excellent." The manager thumped her cane. "But what if you get them wrong? What will you give me, then?"

"Give you?"

"Yes, that's always how riddles work. You answer them right and I give you something. But if you answer them wrong, then I must get something."

"But I don't really have anything to give."

"It doesn't have to be much," the manager said. "I won't ask too much of you if you lose. But rules are rules, and I, and you, must follow them. Believe me, I wish that we didn't have to." She was thinking of her curse.

"I don't know," Sol said. He glanced at Connie. Connie knew he was thinking about losing their bet yesterday, and probably even remembering his failed heat detection device last spring. He didn't know that he wasn't responsible for either of those failures.

"Come on, Sol," Connie said. "You can do it. I know you can. You're so smart." The manager glanced at Connie as she spoke, and Connie felt as if the woman knew everything Connie had ever done—the tricks, too.

"Would you like to hear the first riddle?" the manager asked Sol. "You can hear the first before you decide. That much I can do."

"I can hear the first one?"

"Yes. And these riddles—I think it's a good idea if you try them. Then, if you get them right, I can give you a prize."

"Well"—Sol looked at Connie—"I *am* good at riddles. I used to learn them all, when I was younger. Let me hear the first one, then."

"Good!" She pointed her cane at Sol, who took a step back. It was amazing she could wave a big cane around so much in the shop without hitting anything, but then, it was her shop.

"Here it goes," she said. "Listen carefully . . ."

The less you feed it, the bigger it grows.
The poor have a lot of it, but the rich very little.
If it grows enormous, it disappears.
Every person has it sometimes.

RIDDLES THREE

"I KNOW IT," Sol said. "I know this one."

"Then do you want to try them all?"

"Yes," Sol agreed.

"And what's the answer to the first?"

"Hunger. The answer is hunger. The less you give it, the more it grows. The poor have it more than the rich. And if you have too much of it, you die and it disappears."

"Yes, exactly right. Okay, here's the second one . . ."

> *Two people there were in a home,*
> *And no one left the home,*
> *And no one came into the home,*
> *But then there were three.*

"Two people, and then three? And no one came in or left?"

"No."

Sol thought about it, looking up. "And no one came in through a chimney or through pipes or something?"

The manager shook her head.

Sol looked at her.

"I've got it. That's a good one. Children. A child. The two people are the father and mother, and no one comes in or out, but the woman gives birth, and then there are three."

"Excellent! One more, then, and I can give you a prize. Here's the third, listen . . ."

> Unseen and untouchable, still I can be felt,
> I'm something you give,
> Not for a birthday or special occasion,
> But when nothing is deserved.

"Can you repeat that, please?" Sol asked.

She repeated the riddle.

"Unseen and untouchable, but felt? The wind? But it doesn't sound like the wind." Sol pressed his hand against his chin, thinking. "Can I have some time? To answer it?"

"I'm sorry, but you have to answer now to win." She looked around the shop. "I'll go and help my customer, there. But when I'm back I'll need to know the answer."

She walked away, leaning on her cane, to the man washing his sheepdog. He was blow-drying the dog, using a hose that looked a lot like a vacuum cleaner. The dog stood patiently, a bit unhappy but enduring it, as those who are loved will often endure the attentions of those who love them. The manager and the man had a brief, friendly conversation.

Sol said to Connie, "I don't know it. I don't know this one."

"You must, Sol. I know you can work it out."

"Do you know the answer?"

"Me? Are you kidding?"

The manager walked back over then.

"Have you got it?" she asked. "I will need your answer now."

"I don't know," Sol said, disappointed.

The manager seemed surprised, but just for a

moment. She nodded. "But you tried, didn't you." She spoke half to herself. "That's worth something. It must be." She stepped down an aisle and, reaching into a shelf, pulled out a box and took something out of it. "Here, I can give you this. It's just a small thing." She pushed it into his hand, closing his fingers over it.

Sol looked at it. It was a dog treat in the shape of a bone.

"Now," she said, "you will have to do something for me. I told you it wouldn't be anything too hard. I need the tubs cleaned. I hate doing it myself. And since I'm sure your sister would have wanted to share the prize with you, if you'd won, I think she can also share in the work." She thumped her cane, and there was no arguing with her then. "And I have one more thing to ask of you too. You alone. It'll seem simple, but it isn't. This is the favor I now ask of you. *Don't give up.* Don't give up next time."

"Next time I have to answer riddles?"

"Could be, could be not," she said. She looked

around and sighed. Would she ever be free again to really help children like these? "Now, about those tubs."

The manager gave them some cleaning products—nontoxic and all natural, of course—and Sol and Connie got to work on the two bathtubs near the back. The sheepdog's owner helped it jump down.

The manager said to the dog, *"Sitz."*

The dog sat.

"Why do you say *sits* and not *sit*?" Connie asked.

"German," the manager answered. "I train all my dogs in German. It's one of the earliest languages I learned, long ago. Listen. Here's another one." She reached over to a shelf and found a dog toy.

"Bleib," she told the dog, holding her hand out palm forward in a stop signal. She threw the toy and the dog didn't move.

She put her hand down.

"Bring," she commanded. The dog immediately ran, picked up the toy, and brought it back to the manager.

She turned to Connie. "Here's one that's good to know," she said. *"Gib Laut!"*

The dog barked. She patted the dog on the head.

"You would be a good trainer, I think."

"I'd like to learn," Connie said.

"Maybe sometime in the future. Right now, you've got work to do." She nodded at the tubs.

Sol had already started cleaning. Connie reluctantly joined him. They spent half an hour scrubbing the sides of the tubs and pulling dog hair out of the drains. The manager checked on them once in a while and helped a couple of customers who came in. She also went in and out of the back room, clicking the door shut each time that she did. Connie glimpsed a black cat through that door.

Quantum, she thought. Though it couldn't be.

The manager caught Connie looking.

"What's in there?" Connie asked.

"Do you really want to know? A failed experiment of mine, so far." She opened the door and Connie stepped in, the manager right behind her.

A bird cry made Connie look up. There, a thrush walked back and forth on a rafter, looking down, not at Connie or the manager, but at the black cat pacing below it. The cat was smaller than Quantum, Connie decided.

"I'm training that cat to live with this bird, without hunting it. This particular cat, though, has been very stubborn."

"Isn't it the cat's instinct to hunt the bird?" Connie asked.

"People move past their instincts," the manager said. "You don't always follow your instincts, do you? You can choose to do what is right instead of just what feels good. Well, animals can too. I admit, though, some individuals are harder to teach than others. But one day I'll succeed. I have time."

She glanced out a window and suddenly her

expression changed. "For you, though, it's time to go," she said.

She opened the door, waved Sol in, and pushed them out a back doorway onto a small landing with bags of pet food and a mop. A stairway led down into darkness. She came very quickly behind them, even though she had to use her cane. She prodded them down. Suddenly they found themselves in a dark room, surrounded by shadowy shapes.

The manager's figure hovered over them. They could hear her breath. Her hand reached out.

There was a click and a door opened. Light from outside streamed in, making them blink. The manager pushed them out into the back lot.

"*Seid vorsichtig, meine Kinder,*" she called to them from the doorway. "Be careful, children."

Closing the door, the manager walked back upstairs to her shop, leaning on her cane and moving slower.

"Ah, I see Swift needs his bath," she called out, crossing to greet her newest customer, who was just coming in the front door. It was Holaderry and her dog, J. Swift.

Sol and Connie, meanwhile, got back to the spot where Mr. Blink had parked.

The car wasn't there.

"That's weird," Connie said.

They walked up and down the block on both sides of the street.

"I remember exactly where we parked," Sol said. "It was here, definitely." He stood next to an empty parking spot.

CHAPTER

AN ADMISSION

"WE WERE TOO long," Connie said. "He's gone. We're lost, lost forever! How will we find our way home?"

"Don't be ridiculous, Connie. You can't get lost in a town like this, even a new town. Not at our age. We could find the police in two minutes and ask them. But we don't even have to." He reached into his back pocket and pulled out a packet of tightly folded papers. "Before we moved, I made sure to print out maps of our new town, some satellite photos, important addresses, and bus routes."

He unfolded the papers and started studying them.

"Oak Lane. See, here it is, and here's our house, the star."

Connie was impressed. Some kids at their old

school would have made fun of Sol and called him a "mad scientist" for printing out so many maps like that. But Connie thought differently. She understood that her brother was smart and thought of things she never could.

Right then she made a decision. She would tell her brother what she had done.

As soon as the time seemed right.

"We can take bus number seventeen," Sol was saying. He traced the route on the map with his finger. "Back on Middle Pass Road."

They went around the corner and found the bus sign: BUS 17, BUS 3. While they waited, Sol stopped a woman walking by.

"Excuse me, can I borrow your phone please?"

"Of course," the woman answered.

Sol called their father. He got the voice mail and left a message.

After a long wait, a bus pulled up, number 17.

They boarded it and Sol watched through the window as it drove away, his map in hand, until he was sure he knew the route. Ten minutes later the bus reached the corner in front of the park where they'd played the day before. They got out.

Across the street was the library.

"We have to find out about Holaderry," Sol said. "I think we should do that before we go home." They crossed the street, climbed the steps, and went inside.

Sol borrowed the library phone to call Mr. Blink again.

He still got the voice mail.

"We made our way home, Dad," Sol said in his message. "We're up at the library on the corner. See you soon." He hung up and gave the phone back.

"That's not good that he just drove away," Connie said. "What was he thinking?"

"Maybe there was an emergency," Sol said. Although he didn't really sound convinced.

They checked the computers in the children's section, but those still weren't working, so they walked through the bookshelf aisles to the side where the regular Internet computers stood in a row. Many people used them, book bags and purses placed by their feet.

Sol signed up for the next available one. They would research Holaderry online.

While they waited, Sol and Connie talked quietly about what they would have done if they'd really been lost, without Sol's maps.

"What if you were lost in a big city?" Sol posed.

"I'd find the police," Connie said. "There are a lot of police in cities. I'd go up to one and tell him, or her, what I needed."

"And what if you were lost in the mountains?"

"And I didn't have a cell phone?"

"No."

"Find shelter," Connie said. "Dig a hole to keep warm, collect food. I get to have one candy bar with me," she added, deciding the rules of this game. "I'd eat exactly one fifth of the bar each day." Connie was being mathematical, like Sol.

Sol fell quiet for a moment, looking around the library.

"Sol," Connie said suddenly, a different tone in her voice.

Sol heard the change.

"Yes?" he asked curiously.

"You know that bet we had yesterday?"

Sol nodded.

"I cheated," Connie blurted out quickly before she could stop herself. "I filled the glass with water. You were right about it."

"What?" His voice rose a little, although he seemed to remember that he was still in a library. "How could you have done that?"

"I'm sorry, Sol."

Connie wasn't sure that she felt so much better than before. Wasn't she supposed to feel better?

Sol was glaring at Connie. Another look, though, slowly came onto his face. "I was right? I was right about the ice?" He sounded slightly less upset. "I knew it," he whispered.

A computer freed up then, and Sol, who was watching, stood right away and grabbed the seat before they lost their spot. Connie pulled up a chair, and they got online. Sol gave Connie one more look, pushing his lips out, which he did as a kind of sarcastic expression. About her cheating, she knew. But that look also meant that he'd forgiven her. Then he turned to the computer screen and got caught up in his research.

Sol searched online for information on *Fay Holaderry*.

He looked for records of research scientists in the area, college professors, and doctors. But nothing turned up except for genealogical information—lists of names, births, and deaths.

Sol did turn up a few photos in old editions of the town newspaper, the *Grand Creek Mirror*, which had been archived online. There were photos of someone with the same name, Holaderry, at the raising of the town hall.

But the town hall had been raised more than a hundred years ago—one hundred four years, to be exact. In one photo, the woman with the name Holaderry was sitting in one of the original cars built at that time.

The photo was captioned MRS. HOLADERRY IN HER MOTOR CAR.

Another photo, captioned simply SPECTATORS WATCH, didn't mention Holaderry by name, but there she was in the front row.

"That looks just like her," Sol said.

"It can't be," Connie answered.

Sol searched more in the newspaper archives and, knowing now where to look, dug up a mention of a Mrs. Holaderry in an article from 1873. There was a very old photograph, all gray-hued from the tintype process used back then. Holaderry posed straight-faced. Her hair, twisted into a bun, looked like a funny teapot, if her ears had been two handles.

Staring into those eyes in the photograph, Connie knew it was the same woman she had met the day before.

Sol spent more time searching but came up with nothing else. He printed the photos and the article. After he had collected the pages from the printer, he signed off.

"We need more information," Sol said. "Something very strange is going on."

"But that's all there was," Connie said.

Sol nodded.

"There are other ways to get information. Let's go home."

On the walk down the block, Sol was quiet and seemed to be thinking. Then he suddenly said, as if they'd been talking about it the whole time, "*That's* the answer to the third riddle. Something you give when it isn't deserved. 'Give' is the clue. The answer has that word in it. It's *forgiveness.* Something you give when it isn't deserved, that can't be seen or touched, but felt."

"You see, I knew it," Connie said. "You're super clever. But, you should've thought of it before we had to scrub out those bathtubs."

They neared their new home. Across the street, they saw Holaderry getting out of her car and going into her house with Swift.

Sol pulled Connie to a stop, holding her arm, and they hid the best they could behind a telephone pole.

Holaderry came out right after, alone, got into her car, and drove away, in the opposite direction.

"We've got to get inside that house, Connie.

And we should do it now. This might be the only chance we get."

Connie had an idea that that was what her brother had been planning. She wasn't at all surprised to hear it. She stared at the house and nodded. "Okay," she agreed. "Let's go in."

CHAPTER

INTO THE HOUSE

MEANWHILE, BACK at the apartment, Mr. and Mrs. Blink dug into a huge meal, with candles lit and soft music playing. It looked like they were celebrating.

Mr. Blink pursed his lips as if he'd just remembered something and snapped his fingers. "I should call the babysitter and cancel for tomorrow." He searched for his cell phone, found it in the bedroom, and came back out. "Two messages?" He put the phone to his ear and listened. He looked disappointed.

"Let me guess," Mrs. Blink said.

"That, um—son of mine is too smart for his own good. I don't know how he does it. I had a lot of trouble finding that place this morning. It's easy enough to get lost around here. At least, it was easy for me."

"He's smart enough for his own good, honey. Just not for yours."

Mr. Blink sighed and seemed upset. "I never do anything right."

Mrs. Blink tilted her head. She looked surprisingly sympathetic. She went over and squeezed Mr. Blink's shoulders.

"You're not the brightest bulb in the world, but you're my bulb. My dim bulb. I guess we should clear away the dinner."

"Yep, I guess they'll be back soon."

"Keep the babysitter for tomorrow. We'll still go out for the day. And don't worry so much," she said. "The children will never last long in this town."

SOL and Connie snuck around to the back of Holaderry's house. A rake leaned into the trellis where vines grew up the house's side. A hose was coiled like a snake beside it. They walked around the hose into the backyard.

Barks sounded inside as Sol stepped up to the back door.

"He's a nice dog, and he knows us," Connie said to Sol.

Sol nodded. He thought the same. Swift didn't seem like much of a guard dog. But you never could be too careful.

Sol started searching for a key hidden near the door, under rocks, and behind hedges. "Usually there's a spare key somewhere."

Meanwhile, Connie turned the knob. "It's open," she pointed out.

Sol moved in front of Connie at once. As older brother, he had to go first. He pushed the door open a crack until he could see Swift, who'd stopped barking and started whining.

"It's okay, Swift. It's just us," Sol said. He opened the door farther and let Swift smell his hand. Swift licked it. Sol remembered the dog treat he had in his pocket and fished it out. It had broken into three pieces.

"Here." He gave Swift two of the pieces, which Swift swallowed in seconds. Sol put the last piece back in his pocket. "That one's for later," he said.

He opened the door all the way and he and Connie stepped into the kitchen. He closed the door quietly, while Connie scratched Swift's head.

"We have to hurry. We don't know when she'll be back," Sol said.

"She drove away," Connie said. "She's probably out shopping. She could be gone for hours."

"You never know."

"An hour at least," Connie said.

"Then that's how long we have to figure out exactly who she is."

Scratching Swift behind the ears, Connie said to the dog, "Too bad you can't tell us."

Swift leaned into Connie. Connie interpreted that as *Just keep scratching*.

The kitchen held nothing of interest and no clues about the owner. Except that two teacups by the sink suggested a visitor had been by. Sol remembered the man with the weird little head who'd left the house earlier.

Crossing the kitchen and stepping into the living room, they saw that Holaderry was definitely up to something strange. The room looked like an indoor garden. Herbs hung drying upside down along the walls. Surrounding antique furniture were plants of strange varieties in pots. Little signs,

stuck in their soil, said things like GOOD FOR ARTHRITIS, SWEET DREAMS, and SMELL ME.

With Swift beside her, Connie went over to that last one, a tall red flower shaped like a bell, and she breathed the scent in deeply.

"Connie, get away from there." Sol's voice came to her, very close. Sol had run up and was next to her, pushing her away from the plant.

Sol couldn't help but put his own head near the flower's red bulb as he pushed Connie away. He got a small whiff. It made him giggle.

"We don't know what these plants are," he said.

"It smells so nice, Sol," Connie said, "like . . . like . . ."

Connie couldn't think of what it smelled like, but it was something very funny. She stuck her face near Swift's nose. He licked her. Swift was a very funny dog, Connie suddenly realized.

She started laughing and couldn't stop, kind of like when she stayed up late at night and got giddy.

Sol watched her. Connie was hopping around the room.

"Something's wrong," Sol said, feeling like

laughing too. "We don't have much time; we've got to find out more."

Connie got on her hands and knees next to Swift.

"I'm a doggy too, Sol."

She barked.

Swift licked her face.

She licked his face back. Then she pretended to be a dog peeing.

"Connie! Something's happened to you," Sol said. But he giggled as he said it.

Connie stopped pretending to be a dog, stood, and stuck her pointer finger up her nose.

"Connie, look," Sol said.

He stuck his finger up his nose.

They broke into howls of laughter.

Sol tried to calm himself.

"Wait, Connie, come on, we've got to check upstairs. There'll be something in her bedroom that can tell us more."

Connie's eyes showed that deep inside she understood what Sol was saying. She screamed, "Upstairs!" and sprinted past Sol into the hallway and up the steps. She made a lot of noise running.

Sol followed, trying not to giggle. Swift came beside him. They kept close behind and followed her into a room at the top of the stairs. It turned out to be Holaderry's master bedroom.

The bedroom wasn't huge, but it had a feeling of old-time luxury. Giant square pillows lay across the bed, and Holaderry's dresser had three mirrors on it in a curving shape, so that you could see your face from every angle.

Connie immediately dove onto the bed. Swift jumped up after her. Connie barked, on her knees, while scratching Swift behind the ears. She found a ball by the side of the bed and threw it. Swift jumped off the bed, fetched the ball, and brought it back. Connie took the ball from him and tried to put it in her mouth.

Sol laughed. He couldn't stop himself, though he tried. He started going through Holaderry's dresser. Photos showed a woman who looked like Holaderry—who *was* Holaderry, he thought— in olden times. A very old, framed sketch of Holaderry—from before the time of photographs— showed her younger and thinner. The sketch looked old enough to hang in a museum.

Sol opened the bottom drawer of the dresser and found old letters in handmade envelopes once sealed with wax. He read one that started with "To my Dearest, Horrible Friend Holaderry . . ." That seemed funny to Sol. He took out the letter and put it on the top of the dresser by a small silver box, which he opened. Inside the box was jewelry: earrings, bracelets, rare stones, and a pearl necklace. This last he pulled out and—he had to—put over his head and around his neck, admiring himself in the mirror.

Connie looked over at Sol with the pearl necklace on and laughed.

"Look at me," she said.

Acting like a dog on all fours, she sniffed near Swift's behind.

Sol took lipstick from in front of the mirror and spread it on his lips, giggling. He showed Connie and they both laughed.

Sol picked up tortoiseshell glasses next and put them on. Suddenly, everything changed. What he saw was no longer the bedroom, but the central room in a very old farmhouse cottage. He walked across this imaginary room. A pot hung in the fireplace on a hook. He went and looked out the window—there was no glass—and saw a field of wildflowers, and beyond that, the woods.

He took the glasses off.

He was standing by the bedroom window, staring out at the apartment building where he and Connie now lived.

"Connie," he said, "we've got to get out of here."

Connie was lying on the bed scratching Swift's belly. She rolled onto her back with her hands and legs in the air.

"Come on, Swift. Now you scratch my belly."

Swift licked her face instead.

Suddenly, there was the sound from outside of a car door slamming. Swift's ears perked up and he wagged his tail. He jumped off the bed and ran out of the bedroom.

Sol grabbed Connie. Abruptly, things didn't seem so funny to him anymore.

"We've got to go," he said in a frantic whisper.

He pulled her through a doorway into a sort of study. A leather chair stood by a desk. On the desk was an old notebook. Sol held tight to Connie, who was still laughing in a silly way. They heard the front door open.

Trapped, Sol thought. They were trapped upstairs. Sol went to the window. Letting go of Connie, he pulled at the window until it opened. He stuck his head out. The trellis with vines was beside his head, outside.

He pulled back in and turned to Connie. "Do you think you can climb down the trellis?"

"Of course," Connie said, a huge grin on her face. "What's a trellis?" She giggled. She looked out the window. "I'm a great climber," she said.

Sol knew it was true. And she was lighter than him. If only one of them made it out, it would be her. If he went first, the trellis might break.

"Go, Connie, go." He pushed her toward escape. "Be careful."

Connie leaned out. "No problem," she called back.

"Shh," Sol said.

Connie carefully put one leg out. Sol held on to her other leg, making sure she couldn't fall.

"I've got it," Connie said.

Sol let go, keeping his arm near her torso just in case. Connie pulled herself out easily and stood on the trellis as if it were a ladder.

"Go," Sol whispered.

Connie clambered down the trellis easily. At the bottom she looked up at Sol.

Sol had a thought. He came away from the window, grabbed the old notebook off the desk, and threw it down to Connie.

"Run, Connie, run," he said as loudly as he dared.

Connie picked up the notebook and ran.

Sol heard footsteps coming up the stairs, and Swift's quick clipping paws coming too. In a second Swift would run in.

Sol leaned out the window and took hold of the trellis with one hand. There was no time to worry if it would hold him. In one motion, he pulled himself out the window, clutching the trellis and pulling his arms in, the vine leaves pushing against his face and blocking out all view. He felt the trellis pulling away from the house, and thought for a second that it would pull out completely and he would fall backward. But the trellis held, slightly, at least. Quickly, he climbed down, trying not to step too hard each time he stepped down to the next slat. When he felt near enough to the bottom—looking down he could see he was still very high—he leaped off. He landed tumbling, hurting his shoulder and arm.

Sol looked up and saw Holaderry standing in the window watching him.

He scrambled to his feet and ran.

THE WITCH'S HELPERS

HOLADERRY WATCHED from her upstairs study as Sol ran out of the yard. Had his sister been with him? Holaderry thought from small signs that she had. They were exceptional children to have made it past her magical plants, out of her bedroom, and who knew what else they'd found? And climbing out the window. That showed bravery.

Holaderry scratched Swift's head.

"When was the last time children came into my house and made it out?

I can't even remember. They were in town today too, I'm sure. Well, we missed them twice, but third time's lucky, right?" She snorted. "Next time, Swift, I guarantee they won't make it."

Holaderry went downstairs without looking too closely around her study. But when she came back later to write in her journal, it was missing.

Had she picked it up before and laid it down somewhere odd? She looked over the house, and eliminated all of the possibilities for where it might have been. She realized, only then, what had happened to it.

I love children. Eating them, that is.

I've eaten quite a few children over the centuries. . . .

I have a network of helpers all over the world. They're little creatures, a foot high with squeaky voices, but disguised by their magic you'd never be able to tell the difference between them and real humans. Unless, that is, you knew the secret way to see through their tricks. But you don't, do you?

What a shame.

My little helpers take care of any problems that arise for me. I remember Lily Featherwell, for instance. Now, she was a problem. Lily wrapped up her younger brother, Maurice, very thoroughly, and wrote a note on the computer.

"Please take our son, he is always tattling on his older sister, who is an angel," she typed, printing it out and signing her parents' names. Then she made a call for pickup using my secret pickup system, which she was clever enough to find out.

Well, my helpers take care of all of my pickups, and they were almost fooled, except that Lily got carried away and tried to watch them through the banister upstairs. They have a sixth sense and quickly realized what was happening.

They had to turn down the package then. Because I only accept donations through the proper channels.

Despite this refusal, however, my helpers were called back to the very same house just a few weeks later. This time Maurice had managed to package up Lily. He'd written, by hand, a much more honest note than his older sister's.

"Come on, you can take her. I want her bedroom," he wrote. "It's a lot bigger than mine. And I'm really the nicer one."

A likely story.

My helpers were, frankly, a little upset, because they love to annoy children and they don't like it the other way around, when children annoy them. I, on the other hand, appreciated the troubles that Lily and Maurice were having. I know how hard it is to be the older child, and I know the troubles of being a younger child too.

Believe me, I wish I could have eaten them both.

But I understood my helpers' complaints. They have very important work to do annoying children all over the world. They're the ones who thought up those signs that you see at the amusement park, for example, with a line to show how tall you have to be to get on the rides. That simple idea annoyed millions of children all at once—especially the short ones. I admit, it was very clever.

And if you've ever had a teacher who gave you homework over a long holiday, that was probably one of my helpers in disguise too.

They can't stand it when children enjoy the holidays.

My helpers impersonate school principals, babysitters, carnival booth operators, even the heads of big companies. Anyone who can make trouble for kids—the more trouble the better. That's why they help me, of course.

I am sure some of them are reading this now, and so, to them, I'd like to say that I truly appreciate all the help. Where would we all be without the help we give to one another?

I am greatly in my helpers' debt. They've assisted me for many centuries. In olden times you'd meet them disguised as royal huntsmen, friendly old women, carriage drivers on faraway country roads, and, once in a while, a frog or wolf. Children don't understand that as well as they used to. What—or who—waits for them.

Why, one girl found me out not long ago and, amazingly, showed up on my doorstep.

"I want to learn to be a witch," she said. "All the spells, and creeping out at midnight."

Times have really changed.

In that rare case, I had to make an exception to my rule about receiving donations through the proper channels.

My hideout, after all, must be kept secret.

So I sighed and said, "Come in."

But something in the way I said it made her think twice, and she ran away very quickly. I found her later, though, and she really did become an evil witch. To my surprise, we're now friends.

There are people who oppose me too, around from olden times.

But by taking away something beloved of theirs, and knowing the right words, I have cursed them and they cannot help children anymore. . . .

SOL and Connie sat up all through the night reading those parts—and many others—from Holaderry's journal, Sol often reading aloud to Connie, with only the night table lamp lit.

"She's horrible," Connie said. And later, in a rare moment of helplessness, "Sol, what are we going to do?"

Sol's intelligent eyes had clouded over, as if he wasn't all there.

"Don't lose it now, Sol," Connie said. "I need you."

"What?" Sol asked.

"It seemed like you were far away," Connie said.

He rubbed his eyes. "Just thinking. And a bit sleepy, I guess. Holaderry saw me, Connie. Running away. She was at the window when I got to the ground."

"Do you think Dad would believe us if we told him?"

"I'm not sure we should mention this to Dad."

Neither said more on that topic.

"She must know by now that we took her diary," Connie said. "She'll be after us."

"Yes," Sol said, "logically speaking, there's really only one thing we can do." He looked at Connie, uncertainty in his eyes. "We've got to get her, before she gets us."

CHAPTER

CAPTURED

Wednesday

WHEN SOL AND CONNIE got up that morning, Mr. and Mrs. Blink were gone and the babysitter was sitting at the kitchen table. She was an elderly woman, short and thin, with bony arms. Her gnarled hands held the day's newspaper.

"This morning you'll have to occupy yourselves, however you can," she said to Sol and Connie. "But I'll tell you what." She held up the newspaper. "We'll go to a noon matinee. I know kids always love to see a movie."

Her wrinkled lips pulled back into a smile. Then she put on her glasses, which hung from a chain around her neck, picked up a pencil, and started work on the crossword puzzle. It didn't look likely that she was going to move from that position anytime soon.

Sol and Connie had decided the night before that they would spend the morning figuring out how to handle the terrible situation. But having stayed up all night, sleep got the better of them and they crawled back into bed.

The next thing they knew, the old lady was dragging them out of bed. Sol had a moment of panic, half-asleep, when he imagined it was Holaderry herself pulling on him.

"No! No!" he shouted as he woke up.

"What's the matter?" said the babysitter. "You'd think I was some ogre come to get you. Hurry up. The movie starts soon and it's across town. And I'm not a fast driver."

It turned out the babysitter wasn't exaggerating about her driving. They didn't drive so much as drift across Grand Creek. She braked ahead of the stop signs, waited for the longest time, then crept forward again and braked a second time when they actually reached the intersection. Then she glided across the intersection so slowly that cars going the other way stacked up in a long line, waiting.

Sol, sitting in the front seat, turned to Connie in the back seat and mouthed the word *movies*.

Connie nodded. She knew what he meant. The movie theater was where Holaderry kept her drop-off boxes. They'd read it in her journal.

For all they knew, this new babysitter wasn't a real babysitter at all, but one of Holaderry's helpers, put on the job to dispose of them. They had to be on their guard.

Once they took their seats at the theater, the babysitter went out to the lobby and brought back popcorn and soda. She handed the treats to them.

"Here, Sol, you have some first," Connie said, pretending to be polite, though she didn't fool her brother for a minute.

Sol hesitated over the soda, then finally took a sip. They both waited.

Nothing happened.

Next Sol tried the popcorn. He nodded to Connie. "It's okay," he whispered. "Just a bit salty."

Having let her older brother be the guinea

pig—which was fitting for older brothers, after all—
Connie dug into the treats with relish. She ate
more than her fair share of popcorn during the
movie. And, since that made her more thirsty than
Sol, she also drank most of the soda.

It should be noted that the babysitter had cho-
sen a movie rated for thirteen-year-olds and up,
which Connie wasn't normally allowed to see. The
film wasn't very good, but as it ended and the cred-
its were rolling, Connie said that it was the "best
movie ever," "very funny," one of her "favorites,"
and that she wanted to see many more PG-13
movies as soon as possible.

Meanwhile, the babysitter stood up and started
moving toward one of the side exits at the bottom
of the aisle.

"Let's go out the way we came in," Sol suggested, "through the main exit."

"Going up is just too much for my old bones," the babysitter said. "And look at that crowd. This is much faster."

So they followed her, and the exit door led, just as the children feared, to a side alley, cut off from view of the parking lot. Only a few other people were using the same exit. Sol and Connie walked just a little bit behind the sitter. Looming ahead of them in the alleyway was a big metal bin.

"Why, what's this, I wonder?" said the babysitter as they approached it. "It just says DONATIONS."

Sol and Connie nearly had a heart attack. This was it. It was one of Holaderry's child drop-off boxes, before their very eyes. Even as they saw it, the babysitter slowly turned toward them.

"No!" Sol shouted. "No! You won't get us." He launched himself at her and, feeling stronger than usual, seized her in a bear hug. Luckily, she was light. Connie, in time with her brother, grabbed the old lady's legs, and they heaved her up and into the metal box. The babysitter fell into the box with a clang. Her confused cry of "Help" came out more

like a peep than a shout, just as the door swung shut after her.

"Run!" cried Connie, and they sprinted out of the alleyway into the movie theater parking lot.

Sol and Connie were able to catch a bus back across town. They were red in the face and both breathing heavily. They watched the passengers around them, noticing every person who crossed his legs or scratched her face or did anything at all.

Sol took out his maps and followed their route.

"We should get off here," he said. They descended and were on the same stretch of road they'd been on the day before. "We can take the same bus back as yesterday," Sol explained, "bus number seventeen."

Someone walked out of a shop behind them and called out.

"How nice to see you!" The manager of All Creatures, Big and Small came down the road, surrounded by four dogs who walked without leashes but kept by her side. "How good to see you two again," she said, stopping beside them. The dogs stopped with her. She leaned on her cane, looking down from her great height.

"We're kind of in a hurry," Sol said, not sure what to tell her. He couldn't even be sure that she wasn't one of Holaderry's helpers. Although he didn't get that feeling.

Suddenly Sol remembered something. "I solved your last riddle," he told her. "Forgiveness. The answer is forgiveness."

"Excellent." She raised her cane into the air, leaning on her good leg. "But it's too late for prizes. It's all up to you now. I can only wish you the best. Let's walk." She nodded in the direction the children had been walking. "Where were you going?"

"To the bus stop," Connie said.

The manager nodded. *"Fooss,"* she said to the dogs, or at least that's what the word sounded like. The dogs kept pace with her perfectly as she walked, two on each side. "Come, let's catch your bus."

The number 17 bus was pulling up to the stop. The manager went as fast as she could, the dogs beside her, Sol and Connie running ahead.

It was too short of a time for Connie. She wanted to talk to this woman more. She wanted to tell her that she was interested in being a vet and curing animals, or maybe being a park ranger.

"Have you got the bird and the cat to live together?" she blurted out instead.

"Not yet, but I will." The woman sounded certain.

Sol waited for Connie to board the bus, then got on behind her. "Thanks," he said to the woman, turning back to her.

"Good luck," she told him.

They rode the bus along the same route as the day before and got off when it reached the park on the corner of their block.

"If we go home, we have to pass her house," Connie said.

"And she might be watching for us, no matter which way we go," Sol said. "Let's go to the library first. We can plan from there."

They had just reached the signpost of the library and went in to sit in the children's section.

"Sol, what if the babysitter wasn't really going to throw us in?"

"We did what we had to do," Sol said, uttering an excuse given by many good people who have done wrong over the years. Then he added another commonly used phrase: "We had no choice."

"Yes," Connie agreed. She seemed to feel better hearing that excuse. "We had no choice," she said loudly.

"Shh," said a librarian passing by. It was the same librarian—with the rosy cheeks and all-knowing eyes—who had scolded Connie the other day. "Please, this is a place for reading, not talking," the librarian said as she walked on.

"What if you talk aloud to yourself in order to read? Huh, what then?" Connie said to the librarian's back, but more quietly.

"Connie, calm down. She's just doing her job. The question is, what are *we* going to do?"

"We need some sort of trap," Connie said. "You know, we tie a kid to a stake in the park, wait until Holaderry comes along, and when she goes for the kid, we catch her. Like how they leave goats tied to stakes to catch tigers."

"We can't tie any kids to stakes, Connie. But . . ." Sol didn't continue.

"But . . . we could use one of us as bait,"

Connie said, picking up on her brother's thoughts. "Or we could sacrifice one of ourselves completely. Eat something she's allergic to, let her catch us and eat us, and then she'll die too."

"That's not exactly a good plan. But the first one is. We let her think she's got us, then we get her." Sol put his hand to his chin. It was a sign that he was thinking hard. "Look," he said, "maybe I've got a few ideas. Let me go online for a minute, check some things out. You stay here. Don't go anywhere."

"Where would I go?"

Sol went to the Internet computers. He signed up and got online right away. He searched everywhere to find the Web pages he needed, somewhere out there.

But sometimes out there, far away, is the wrong place to look for what one needs.

Meanwhile, Connie got up from her seat in the children's section and looked at books. As she did, she thought about what would happen if she and Sol didn't make it. She realized that she'd regret not telling Sol the truth.

Even if it had been a mistake.

Connie remembered sneaking into Sol's room the night before the science fair. Sol had been out in the backyard looking through his telescope, probably imagining himself on another planet. Sol belonged on another planet somewhere, thought Connie.

Sol's bedroom light had been on. Connie knew that he kept his science fair invention locked in the closet. He'd known his sister would try to look at it sometime. But as usual Sol wasn't clever enough for Connie. She knew nearly all of his hiding places and she'd found the padlock key almost immediately, put the key in the lock, and the lock sprang open.

She thought to go and peer out Sol's bedroom window to check on Sol, then stepped back over to the closet and dragged out his invention. She shouldn't have done it, but Sol keeping it secret had only made her want to see it more. The invention stood on a stand, had a small satellite dish attached to the front, and a computer screen. When she turned it on, it showed some fuzzy red and yellow blobs, and the words HOT WATER HEATER.

She couldn't tell what it was, but she could tell it was good. She turned it off and opened the side panel, because one of the screws was loose, and, well, it practically opened by itself.

Many layers of circuit boards were stacked one over the other.

Connie tried to put the side on again, and that's when one of the computer chips fell out from a bottom layer.

"Oh no, drat, drat, drat," she whispered.

She did her best to put it back, but it wouldn't hold in place. She got it in exactly the way she thought it must go, touching the next chip, and used the only thing she had to make it stay where it was, a bit of her gum, which she was chewing on right then. She was careful to stick the gum where it didn't touch any of the electronics.

Connie admired her ingenuity—she was clever at the quick fix. She got the side on, pushed the invention back in the closet, locked it, and left quickly, walking into the kitchen. Sol was just coming in from the backyard.

There was no way for him to know that she'd been in his room.

That night Connie worried.

"He'll check it. He'll test it," she told herself. Of course he would, she thought.

She didn't know that he'd already run the invention through its final check.

The next morning at the science fair, Sol had come to see Connie's exhibit in the school hallway and she'd tried to suggest that he check his invention one more time. But he hadn't taken the hint. He'd gone out to do his presentation for the whole school, and Connie had watched it go horribly wrong.

She had been too chicken, then, to tell him. He would never have forgiven her for doing such a thing.

Connie felt like she had to tell Sol now, though, even if she was still a little scared to do it.

She took some books about animals off the children's shelf, thinking of the All Creatures manager and wondering if the woman really loved all creatures, big and small, even fierce ones like crocodiles and sharks. Connie thought the answer was yes.

One of the books Connie looked at opened to

pictures of camels, and she read something she'd never heard before, that camels sometimes spit on people. And there were photos of another animal, called a llama, that also "spit as far as fifteen feet," according to the book. "Llamas spit at other llamas to control the herd," the book said. "Llama spit can be green from stomach fluids."

Could you love an animal that spit green gunk on you? Connie wondered. That made her want to laugh. She looked at the llama and camel photos and began to laugh. Not like when she'd been in Holaderry's house, laughing in that weird way, just normal everyday laughter.

Connie saw the librarian coming toward her. Still, she laughed louder.

"You must be quiet!" the librarian said in a hushed command.

Another time, Connie might have apologized. But she wasn't in the mood to do it, and certainly not to this woman. If Connie couldn't laugh at this world—and at animals that spit at one another— then what was there left to do? She opened her mouth and cackled right in the librarian's face.

"That's it. You must leave right now. I won't have you in this library disturbing others."

"But . . . but . . ." Connie wanted to say that her brother was coming back for her.

The librarian took her by the arm and led her to the back of the stacks, where there was a small door marked EXIT with what looked like a hand-painted sign. She opened the door and pointed.

"March," she ordered.

The room was dark. The librarian shoved Connie in and then came in herself. She flicked a switch and a yellowish bulb lit the room. Hanging on the wall was a large canvas bag and a coil of rope. She threw the bag over Connie's head.

She was one of Holaderry's helpers. "All these days," she said, "having to put up with you kids. You run around the library like it's a playground. And you lose your library cards every other week!" She wrapped the rope around Connie, who struggled fiercely but wasn't strong enough to escape the helper's surprisingly strong grasp. "And with a whole library full of books, row after row after row, aisle after aisle, thousands of books, what do you want to read? Books based on TV programs! Unbelievable. What about the deeply moving book we bought last year that shows what life was like for a Berber girl during the Middle Ages? Did you look at that one? What about the terrific book we have for you kids about Gandhi and *ahimsa*? Do you care?"

"But I'm the one who asked you about *War and Peace* and *Wuthering Heights*, remember?" Connie shouted from inside the sack.

The helper paused. "True."

"You should let me go then."

"Mmm, if you'd said *Middlemarch* and *Remembrance of Things Past*, I just might have."

That was bad luck for Connie. The helper continued, "And will you kids stop reshelving books? Leave them on the table."

She finished. Connie was tied up in the sack on the floor like a bag of potatoes. She started shouting but the helper was prepared for that. The sack was specially made for catching kids. One tap on the cloth and all sound from inside was muffled.

"Shh! Please, this is a library," the helper said.

"Remember to use your library voice." She said the last words in a hushed tone.

The helper stepped back into the library aisles, straightened herself up, went to the front desk, picked up the phone, and dialed.

After listening for a time, she said, apparently to an answering machine, "Hello, the book you requested is in, Mrs. Holaderry. Please come and pick it up today." She hung up.

Sol came back to the children's books section shortly after. He looked everywhere for Connie but couldn't find her. He went up to the librarian.

"Have you seen my sister? Short hair, wearing a jumper? She was sitting here."

"Oh, yes, I saw her," the librarian said. "She left just a few minutes ago, I believe."

"She left?" Sol sounded surprised. "Did she say where she was going? Did she leave a message for me?"

"No, no message."

"Was she with anyone?"

"No one that I saw."

Sol was amazed. How could Connie leave now? He checked through the aisles just in case the librarian was mistaken. Then he went out by the rear entrance, in time to see a car backed up to the library, and none other than Holaderry herself loading a squirming sack into the trunk. She slammed the trunk shut, got into the car, and drove away, turning onto the road in the direction of her house.

Something about that sack reminded Sol of Connie. He was sure that she was inside. Possibly only someone like an older brother could recognize a younger sister even when she's tied up inside a sack.

Sol felt dizzy for a moment from the shock of what he'd seen. He leaned against the building, his arms extended, his head down, and his eyes closed.

A moment later, he raised his head and opened his eyes to the world. There was only one thing to do now. He wished he didn't have to do it. He really wasn't good at this sort of thing. In fact, he didn't think he had any chance at all.

He raced toward Holaderry's house.

SOL SAW HOLADERRY'S car parked in the driveway. He ducked into a neighboring yard and ran through the garden. Slipping into Holaderry's backyard, breathless, he stepped up to the windows, peering first into the kitchen, then around by the trellis to look into the living room. He expected to see Holaderry and Connie, tied up. Perhaps Holaderry would be preparing a meal.

But the rooms were empty.

He tried the back door into the kitchen. It was unlocked. He rushed in, stopped, listened carefully, but heard nothing. Visions of Connie went through his head. Connie beside a bubbling cauldron. Connie covered with carrots and cabbage, salt and pepper raining down on her.

Staying as quiet as possible, he passed into the living room, that indoor garden. He kept his distance from the plants, especially the flowers. He hurried into the hallway, up the steps, and made it upstairs with little noise. But on the upper landing his foot caught on something sticking out from under a table. The table shook and an ornamental bowl fell off, shattering loudly.

He froze.

No one came out of any of the rooms. There were no shouts, no footsteps. Sol looked down to see what his foot had knocked against. It was one of Swift's toys. Of course, Swift wasn't there either. The dog would have come running right away when Sol had entered the house.

Then where was everyone? Sol went cautiously into the master bedroom. Empty. He didn't try on any clothes or look through the letters or put on those glasses. He passed straight into the study, where he'd stolen the notebook. His glance fell on the window. He didn't want to have to exit through there again. He'd been lucky enough the first time.

The upstairs, it seemed to him, was empty. He

stuck his head into the two other rooms—bathroom and guest room—just to be sure. Nothing.

Where was Connie? The minutes were ticking by. Sol estimated that he'd been searching for more than five minutes already.

He hurried back downstairs and found a door to a cellar. Flicking a switch that lit a single bulb over the steps, he bounded down the creaky staircase. The bulb cast a light over decaying boxes and appliances, stacked unevenly. An old freezer hummed.

Sol pulled the freezer door open. It was full of ice cream of many flavors. Holaderry must love ice cream.

Closing the door, he searched the rest of the cellar as fast as he could. The ancient walls were crumbling. But he discovered no other doors or entryways.

Very frustrated, he ran back upstairs and asked himself: Holaderry's car was in the driveway; she *could* have parked at the house and walked somewhere else, but why? Why would she have driven back here at all? And where else was there to go?

Every second Sol didn't find them was a second during which Connie might be . . . cooked!

One thought crept into his head. It had first occurred to him standing in the cellar. A secret room, or rooms, either between the other rooms or underneath the house, in the cellar, or in some vault below the cellar.

There was something wrong too with the kitchen.

Everything looked normal.

That's what was wrong, Sol finally realized. Holaderry would need special, kid-cooking equipment—humongous ovens, maybe a cauldron, and unique serving dishes. There was none of that here.

Holaderry had another kitchen.

It would be in the house. Sol was sure of it.

Connie, he thought, I'm coming. I'm going to save you.

He rushed from room to room, looking for anything that could have been a secret entrance. He pulled up the carpet in the hallway and looked for cracks in the floor that could reveal a trapdoor.

Upstairs, in the bedroom, he shoved the mattress off the bed to see clearly underneath. He searched for those glasses—maybe they'd reveal something hidden to him—but they were gone. He pushed the dresser away from the wall. Nothing.

Upstairs wasn't the most likely place for a hidden room, anyway. Although he should never assume anything, Sol thought.

Still, he raced two steps at a time back down to the living room. He pushed over the potted plants, holding his nose shut. He tore down the herbs that hung upside down to dry and searched the walls behind them. In the hallway was a small painting of a forest, mountains in the distance, and two sets of footprints leading into the trees. He knocked it down. Nothing was behind it.

He ran downstairs to the cellar again and searched every corner for a hidden door. He pushed the freezer aside, bit by bit—it was very heavy—looking for a trapdoor beneath.

He couldn't find anything.

Sol was frantic.

Where were his smarts now? Running back

upstairs, he opened a closet that he had already searched and took out a hammer he had seen lying among other tools. There were several hammers, actually, and he took the biggest one. He went around the house now and started wildly beating holes in the walls with it. Maybe behind the walls there was a room.

Made of plasterboard, the walls caved in easily. But behind them were only pipes and wires.

All the time Connie's face flashed before him. He was going to fail her, he realized. Her older brother, who should have saved her, was going to fail. He slumped down against the hallway stairs.

What was it the All Creatures woman had asked him to do? Don't give up?

And he *hadn't* given up. But it wasn't enough. He hadn't found Connie or Holaderry. He was a failure. He'd never truly admitted it, but nothing he'd done lately had worked.

And that's when he understood what he needed. The invention he kept, partly disassembled, in that box in the back of his closet. His heat detection device.

If he could get it to work, he could find Holaderry's hidden kitchen.

Sol sprinted out of Holaderry's house and across the yard to his apartment building.

He wasted moments getting his keys to work. Mr. and Mrs. Blink still weren't there. Once in his bedroom, he dove into the closet and pulled out everything, finally getting to the taped-up box in the back. He slid it out and opened it.

Why hadn't it worked?

At last, he did what he hadn't done before. He took apart the last few pieces. And there, staring him in the face, was the problem. A piece of chewing gum, hardened and gray. He lifted it out and smelled it. Zigley's peppermint, he could tell from the very slight odor.

Connie's brand.

Sol's head reeled. Connie couldn't have sabotaged his presentation. She would never have done that. But here was the evidence. He was holding it in his hand. He banged his palm against the floor. The idea flashed through his mind: Let her be eaten.

Why not? What had she ever done for him? She'd always caused trouble. She wanted to be treated like an equal even though she was younger, and he'd done that. He'd never been mean to her, hardly ever.

Sol was wasting time thinking. His eyes fell on a half-unpacked box full of little things Connie liked: a framed photo of a pop star boy band, a plastic figurine of the Monster from the Deep.

I'll save you, Connie, he thought. I may never forgive you, but I'll save you.

He kneeled beside his heat detection device and started rebuilding it.

It wasn't too hard to reassemble the device. Sol was smart enough to bypass the few circuits that had burned out and to determine, under pressure, what he could do without in this emergency case. It only had to work once.

He finished in eight minutes, according to his clock-and-weather predictor. Sol abruptly took that too off the windowsill. He disconnected a few wires and put it on top of his heat detection device so he could carry it all.

Once outside, he stood the heat detection device pointing at Holaderry's house and turned it on.

The screen flickered to life.

Everything read cold, except for one corner below the kitchen, underground as Sol had suspected. That part of the screen glowed bright red, and next to it, on the side, the screen read "Ovens (very hot)." As Sol had designed it, the "very hot" part flashed on and off.

Ovens (very hot).

Ovens.

Ovens (very hot).

CHAPTER

A DIFFERENT WAY OF
THINKING

GRABBING UP HIS clock-and-weather device in his arms, Sol raced across the yard toward the house. He passed the trellis that he and Connie had climbed down and ran around to the back door. He rushed into the kitchen. The floor had a complicated crisscross pattern that was perfect for hiding the edges of a trapdoor. Still, Sol searched every line carefully and could find nothing.

He had to think like a witch. Like Holaderry.

The seconds were ticking, as his clock-and-weather device noted by changing one more minute. He looked around the kitchen. Suddenly he knew. The stove. It had to be the stove.

He went over and tried the burners. None of them lit. It was a fake. The entrance was beneath it.

He pushed with all his strength, but the stove wouldn't budge. He opened the oven door and tried to remove the bottom of the oven. The metal plate did come off with a clang. But there was no entrance beneath.

He stared at the stove.

Think like her, he told himself. Don't think scientifically. Think like your adversary.

He reached out and turned the oven dial to BAKE.

There was a click.

The stove rose off the floor, gears clanking. It slid sideways, and a trapdoor opened to reveal stairs. Sol walked quietly and quickly down into a narrow hall. A huge glass cabinet loomed on one side, full of strange objects: a gilded mirror, a long wood walking stick carved in the shape of a bird, a giant ceramic flower. He crept to the end of the hall, stopping at the verge of a doorway, peered around the doorjamb, and saw Holaderry, in an apron, standing between long stove tops.

Connie was tied to a table near one side.

Swift lay in a corner, sleeping.

Cooking utensils, mixers, soup ladles, wooden

spoons, cheese grat-
ers, whipping cream
whisks, and every-
thing Holaderry
would need to
cook her favorite
meals—and her
favorite kids—hung
from little hooks over
the stoves. A cauldron
leaned against the wall, which was stone like a cave
wall. A fire pit was sunk in the floor past the cauldron.
Smoke rose out of it.

Holaderry had her back to Sol.

Sol calculated the number of steps he'd need to
get to Connie, how long it would take to untie her,
and how quickly they could escape.

"So, you found us." Holaderry still had her
back to Sol. She turned around slowly.

Connie turned her head when she heard the
voice. Swift raised his head also, waking from his nap.
He got up and trotted over to Sol, wagging his tail.

"I didn't think you would," Holaderry said, "but

then you're very clever, aren't you? Good. One more meal for me."

"Sol! Sol! Save me!" Connie shouted. "No, run, Sol!" she decided. "Save yourself!"

Holaderry strode around the front stove, moving toward Sol.

"Not one step closer," Sol shouted at her. He held up his clock-and-weather device with its octopus of wires. Sol had disconnected temperature, barometric pressure, and the weather prediction. The screen read only the time now: **5:03PM**.

"Do you see this?" Sol said. "When the time reaches five-oh-five, if I haven't connected a certain wire on this device, my heat beam invention upstairs is going to start burning all of your old letters that you keep in that dresser in your bedroom. I set up my invention before I came down here. And then your dresser will light, with all its old photos, and soon your whole house will be gone. But I'll bet it's the letters you care about most. Those will go first." Sol stared at her. He must have looked wild. That's how he felt.

Holaderry hesitated. It was clear that Sol had

guessed right. Her letters, some of them from hundreds of years ago, were important to her. She narrowed her eyes. She stared and stared at Sol, while he tried to look as crazy as possible, and then suddenly she smiled.

"It's a nice try," she said. "Maybe after you've lived a few hundred years more, you'll be able to bluff me. But I've seen a lot more than you." She made a move toward Sol, more quickly than Sol thought possible. She seized the clock-and-weather device in one hand and Sol's hair in the other.

"Get her, Sol!" Connie shouted.

Sol struggled fiercely, but he discovered there were disadvantages to having long hair that he hadn't considered before.

Soon he was tied to the table beside Connie. He tried to slide out of the ropes but it was no use.

"It's true!" Connie shouted at the witch. "What he said. He almost burned down the whole school last year. My brother's a real mad scientist. The kids call him the Bad Scientist." The clock-and-weather device had changed to **5:05PM**. "Your letters are burning right now!"

"A likely story," Holaderry said. She went back to the stove. After a few moments, she said, "Now look what you've made me do. I've overcooked the sauce. I'll have to get some more fresh marjoram." She turned the burners down and walked out of the kitchen. They heard her footsteps going up the stairs.

"You did it, Sol. You tricked her. She went up to check her bedroom for sure."

"And what can we do?" Sol asked.

Connie struggled, grunting. "I don't know. But it was a good try."

"I'm sorry," he said. "I couldn't save us." He turned his head until their noses were almost touching. "You know, you really shouldn't have stuck that gum in my heat detection device. You ruined my life."

Connie, who'd had plenty of time to get used to her situation by then, answered, "I know, I felt so bad after. I'm sorry, Sol. But I couldn't tell you after that presentation. You were so upset. It was such a disaster! I thought you'd never forgive me."

"I'm not sure I will."

"Well, you'd better hurry up and decide," Connie said, "because I don't think we have much time left."

She waited a moment. "So?"

"I'm not sure I can forgive you, Connie," Sol said. "I'm just not sure."

Needless to say, that didn't make Connie feel so good. Still, the point right now, she thought, was escape. They had just a minute or two left before Holaderry came back down and started the meal again. Maybe Holaderry did have to get more herbs, after she found that her bedroom was safe. That could buy them a little time.

But there was no way to get out of their ropes.

"Connie," Sol said quietly.

"What?" she asked.

"Swift. Swift is here."

Connie turned her head, the only thing she could move freely, to look over. Swift was watching them from his spot on the stone floor, where he'd settled back down. His ears perked up when he heard his name.

"Swift," Sol called, "help us."

The dog gazed at Sol and Connie curiously.

"Swift, please."

The dog hesitated, then scrambled up and trotted over to them. He jumped up, his front legs on the table, and licked Connie's face.

"Swift, a knife," Connie said between licks, "get us a knife. Fetch," she said. No, that wasn't the word. *"Bring,"* she commanded, remembering the right one.

At once, Swift jumped down. He ran over to a corner of the kitchen, found his ball, and carried it to Connie, happily wagging his tail.

"No, Swift, no," Connie said. "Not the ball. The knife. Over there." Connie tried to point with her head but Swift just watched as Connie's head moved back and forth. He seemed to understand that the ball was the wrong thing, though, and he dropped it and let it roll away.

"Yes, that's it, Swift. Not the ball. The knife. *Bring* the knife," Connie commanded.

Swift looked in different directions. What was there to fetch? He trotted off, sniffing things and looking up at Connie from time to time to see if he was doing right.

"What's the word in German for knife, Sol?"

"I don't know," Sol whispered. He was staying as quiet as he could. Connie needed to get this right, and the sound of his own voice would only confuse Swift. Silently, Sol thought, You can do it, Connie.

Swift trotted by open cabinets stuffed with baking pans and cookie sheets. When the dog reached a magnetic strip, where knives and metal utensils hung, Connie called, "The knife. That's it. *Bring* the knife."

Swift looked at Connie and seemed to understand the tone of her voice. Something was wanted there.

Swift started pulling a pair of barbecue tongs off the magnetic strip. "No, no, not that, Swift." Swift could tell he'd got the wrong thing from Connie's tone of voice. He let go and reached over for another thing on the strip.

"That's it! *Bring.*"

Swift had taken the handle of a large knife in his mouth.

Holaderry could come back at any moment, Connie thought.

"*Bring* it *here*, Swift," Connie said excitedly. She didn't even know that the word for "here" is pronounced the same in German.

Wagging his tail, Swift pulled the knife free from its magnetic holder and came to the table where the children lay.

He jumped up with his front legs on the table-top and looked at Connie, saying with his eyes, "Is this what you wanted? Aren't I a good dog?"

"Quick, Sol, use your hand against mine to get the knife. I can't grab it myself."

Sol and Connie pressed their hands together with the knife blade between them. They were able to hold it that way. Sol got a grip on the handle.

As he cut the ropes, Sol realized that he really had gotten the witch out of the room for a long time with his bluff.

Unfortunately, Sol realized this because he heard, at that moment, Holaderry descending the stairs. He worked frantically at the ropes.

And Holaderry was too late. Sol and Connie were free when she walked into the room.

"No!" she shouted. She seemed to sense, only then, that these two, unlike the ones before them, could defeat her.

Sol was the fastest of the two, by a split second. He reached the witch and pushed his hands into her stomach. She fell on her behind. Connie took the pot of hot sauce from the stove and tossed it over Holaderry's head. Holaderry howled. Still, even as she held her hands over her face, she rose again and loomed over the children. She reached out and almost caught Sol. She was so fast. But Sol was too quick for her this time.

"The pit!" Connie shouted.

The fire pit was behind Holaderry. Sol shoved as hard as he could against her.

The witch fell backward.

There was total surprise in her eyes as she plunged, back first, into the pit. She shrieked. Afterward, there was only smoke rising softly.

Sol and Connie ran out of the room. Swift, who had been barking furiously during the fight—not understanding why it was happening—ran with them into the short hall but hesitated to go up the stairs without Holaderry.

Sol remembered the treat in his pocket. He pulled out that last piece and gave it to Swift, who swallowed it quickly.

Then Swift turned and ran back into the kitchen.

"We should take him with us," Sol said.

"No, that's where he belongs," Connie said. "Someone will rescue him later. Come on."

Sol paused when they passed the huge glass cabinet in the hall, his eye caught by the ancient walking stick that lay inside among the other strange items. A duck's head was carved into the handle of the stick. There was something familiar about that head, he thought.

"Doesn't that cane remind you of someone?" he asked.

Connie nodded. "Definitely."

He opened the cabinet and took the walking stick. Then they went up the steps two by two, into the sunlit kitchen, and sprinted out of the witch's house, believing that they had defeated her.

CHAPTER

THE EXCEPTIONS

SOLOMON AND CONSTANCE Blink trudged up the road. It wound toward the mountains. They carried knapsacks. Sol stopped and took out his water bottle. He took a sip and handed it to Connie, who tipped it up and drank.

"Say, Connie, if I put ice in there and the ice melts, will the water be higher or lower?"

Connie handed back the bottle.

"The same level," she answered quietly.

"Wanna bet?"

"No," Connie said. "No. I don't." She lifted the strap of her bag onto her shoulder and started walking again. Sol walked along with her. "Are you ever going to forgive me?"

"No, I never will. That doesn't mean I won't help and protect you, though."

"I don't need your protection," Connie snapped back. "Just wait till you do something really wrong and you want to be forgiven."

Sol shrugged. He looked back down the road for the hundredth time.

"The bus should come soon," he said.

They had packed their bags quickly, back in their new home, and left without a note. Sol didn't know if Mr. and Mrs. Blink had returned, noticed that Sol, Connie, and the babysitter weren't there, and had gone out again, or if they simply hadn't come back. But it didn't matter. Sol knew enough to understand what had really happened—or at least part of what had really happened. Sol had started to write a note, but he'd thrown it out and closed the door to the apartment behind them without any regret.

I'll never depend on anyone again, not even Connie, he thought. I'm on my own.

But it wasn't true, of course.

He wasn't on his own.

They'd gone to All Creatures, Big and Small looking for help, but the store was closed. New words had been written on the flyer with the riddle

challenge, though, so that it read: ANSWER 3 RID-
DLES AND WIN A PRIZE. *GOOD LUCK, YOU TWO*. Sol
and Connie were sure it was meant for them.

Sol took the walking stick then—he'd been carry-
ing it with him—and leaned it against the shop
door. He had a feeling that the manager could use
it. It seemed to belong there, he thought, and not
in the witch's house. Struck by a thought, he'd
reached into his bag, torn a page out of his notebook, and written "Thank you"
on it. Connie had signed it
along with him, added her
own "Thanks!" and they'd
stuck it on the carved duck
bill at the top of the walking
stick.

There was a bus heading
west over the mountains,
they'd found out in town center, leaving later that day.
But they'd decided
that it was impor-
tant to get away as
quickly as possible.

"We'll walk out of town and wait for the bus at a crossroads," Sol had said.

"Will the bus stop for us?"

"Usually they do, for people who live on the country roads."

That was good enough for Connie. She wanted out.

While they walked down the road, Sol read aloud another section from Holaderry's journal. He'd taken it with him.

Of course, plenty of parents keep their children. It's true.

I remember Ms. Miro. She was the most normal woman in the world, and she liked it when everything was normal around her. If children misbehaved in her presence—being loud in a theater or running down supermarket aisles—she scowled and bossed them around, even in front of their parents.

Then she married a man as normal as herself, and they had a son and daughter of their own.

Their daughter, the younger one, played very rough at school. Even at age six, the girl got into fights. And after watching a motorcycle club dressed all in leather ride by she announced that she would wear only leather clothes from then on. She complained every time she had to put on cotton.

Their son, meanwhile, wanted to stay up after his bedtime every night.

He argued like a lawyer: "I got up two hours late this morning," he reasoned, "so I should be able to stay up two hours late tonight."

He haggled like the world's best salesman: "Just one and a half hours more," he offered. "Okay, one hour. Okay, fine! A measly half hour. You win."

When those strategies didn't work, he went for passive resistance, lying limp, and shouting: "No! I'm never going to bed again!" Until he was carried away.

Every night was the same.

Ms. Miro and her husband didn't understand how normal people like themselves came to have such strange children. They looked at them as two dogs might have looked at their offspring if they'd given birth to kittens.

Still, they tried the best they could to raise their children well. They corrected the children often, and scolded them nearly every day. But they turned down all my offers to take those odd children off their hands.

Oh well, you can't win them all. . . .

SOL stopped reading, looked at Connie—that look between them had all the memories of the past few days in it—and closed the notebook. He would read it all, from start to finish, later on. And he was going to buy history books, sociology books, fiction books, books of all kinds, to put side by side with his scientific books, which he had to buy new again too, since he couldn't carry them with him. Except his mother's scientific treatise—he'd taken that of course.

There was a lot that science alone couldn't answer, Sol realized.

And he wanted to know everything.

He watched the road as they walked, glancing back often. The bus should come soon. They had an aunt who lived west of the mountains. She had always been kind.

They would start with her.

Connie, meanwhile, walked beside Sol, lost in her own thoughts. She was wondering: Were there many families like hers?

Pine trees rose on either side of the road. Connie listened to the birds crying out from the forest. She breathed the fresh air. This was the place for her, she thought.

The great outdoors.

Sol put his arm around Connie's shoulder, and they walked that way for a while, side by side—a brother and sister who'd stuck together in a time of great trial.

CHAPTER

OLD ENOUGH
TO ACCEPT THINGS

Thursday

LIGHT STREAMED OVER the mountains and through the bedroom window. Holaderry gazed at herself in the mirror. She rubbed lotion gently onto her face, then onto her arms, and frowned. She would never look the same again. She had scars on her face, arms, and legs. They looked awful.

Holaderry had lived long enough to accept such a thing, though. She was lucky to be alive. When she was stuck in the fire pit, Swift had come and brought her a tangled rope from a table. She'd been able to use that, with Swift holding tightly to the other end—like in a tug-of-war—to climb out.

Now Swift stood glancing anxiously at her from the bathroom doorway. Since the incident, he'd

been much more nervous. He stuck close to her everywhere she went, always on the watch and jumping at the smallest sound. He ran to her if she so much as groaned or sighed.

As she put on her face cream, Holaderry saw Swift reflected in the mirror, watching her.

She went over to him and patted him on the head.

"It's okay," she said softly. "You didn't know what you were doing." She bent over and scratched Swift behind the ear. "I forgive you."

She stood up straight. "Now, let's see what we've got for supper. I guess it's just tea and cakes tonight. But there's always tomorrow, eh, Swift?"

And the two went downstairs to enjoy their evening meal.

The End

ACKNOWLEDGMENTS

Acknowledgments are due to kindhearted Edward Necarsulmer IV; Christy Ottaviano, for ingeniously guiding me to realize my vision; awesome author Kristin Kladstrup, for early prescient advice and help. Readers and advisers include Stacie Heintze; Shaun Cutts; Ruth, Ben, Louis, Walter, and Sara Teitelbaum; Nancy, Julian, and Nellie; Heather and Jeffrey Lang; Joannie Duris; Jane Hertenstein; Lynne Flanagan; Concord Crit Group; Newton Crit Group; Chicago Crit Group. Help came from Carrel Muller Gueringer; SCBWI LA (God bless New Orleans); Esther Hershenhorn; Esme Codell; everyone there in SCBWI IL; SCBWI New England; Nike; Karl, Kit, Harris, and Miss Katie. Many thanks to librarians in Somerville, Cambridge,

Newton, and Boston, Massachusetts; New Orleans; Chicago (especially Bezazian, Uptown, Sulzer, Harold Washington); and Vienna. Of course, Carla, Jeff, Benny, Simcha, Seth, Kathy, Ethan, and Jacob McGowan; Paul McGowan, rest in peace; Judee Rosenbaum; Johanna Striar; and for encouragement, getting me started, and keeping me going, Kim Sobel. Finally, Kelly Joyce has read every word I've ever written, given advice, editing, guidance, and support.

ABOUT THE AUTHOR

Keith McGowan has worked most of his life as an educator. He helped run an elementary after-school program and day camp, taught mathematics and science, volunteered for a year as a teacher in Haiti, and tutored students who were unable to attend school full time. An avid traveler, Keith began writing *The Witch's Guide to Cooking with Children* in Amritsar and Himachal Pradesh, India, staring at the Himalayan mountains, and continued working on it in Boston, New Orleans, Chicago, and Vienna, Austria, where he now lives with his wife. This is his first novel for young readers.